Maggie
Forevermore

Maggie Forevermore

JOAN LOWERY NIXON

Harcourt Brace Jovanovich, Publishers

San Diego   New York   London

Requests for permission to make copies
of any part of the work should be mailed to:
Permissions, Harcourt Brace Jovanovich, Publishers,
Orlando, Florida 32887.

Library of Congress Cataloging-in-Publication Data

Nixon, Joan Lowery.
Maggie forevermore.

Summary: Happy living with her Texas grandmother
and looking forward to celebrating a family Christmas,
thirteen-year-old Maggie is devastated when she is
summoned by her movie-director father to spend Christmas
with him and her very young stepmother in California.
[1. Fathers and daughters—Fiction.
2. Christmas—Fiction.
3. Motion picture industry—Fiction.
4. Stepmothers—Fiction] I. Title.
PZ7.N65Mae 1987   [Fic]   86-20135
ISBN 0-15-250345-5

Designed by Michael Farmer
Printed in the United States of America
First edition
A B C D E

For my friend and editor
Pamela Susan Tehrani

Maggie
Forevermore

Maggie Ledoux sat cross-legged below the Christmas tree and cradled a shimmering, hand-painted glass ornament. "What story do you have for this one, Grandma?" she asked.

Grandma, stretching to loop a glittery rope of tinsel on a top branch, peered over her shoulder. "Your grandpa and I bought that one in Germany," she said. "We wandered down a mysterious little alleyway and got lost from our tour group. A shopkeeper suddenly popped out of a doorway, then surprised us by giving us directions and fresh gingerbread. We bought the ornament as a way of saying 'thank you.'"

Maggie's best friend, Lisa, crawled over to examine the ornament. "You've got a story to go with every single one of your ornaments," she said. "This is the most interesting Christmas tree I ever helped decorate."

"You haven't helped much," Maggie teased Lisa. "You've been playing with the windup Santa Clauses and eating the peppermint candy canes."

"Only two," Lisa said as she reached for the nearest limb. "Watch. I'll hang the rest on the tree."

"Hang the candy canes up high," Grandma said. "If they're on the lower branches, where the little children and Flowerpot can reach, they'll soon disappear."

Maggie stood and surveyed the tree. "If they're all up high, the tree is going to look lopsided."

"It's going to look lopsided anyway," Grandma said. She stepped back and grinned at Maggie. "Every year the Christmas tree holds more and more ornaments and looks more and more cluttered."

"Not cluttered. Colorful," Maggie said.

Lisa stood with them, dusting off her knees. "Maybe the word is 'gaudy,' " she said.

"I love it!" Maggie insisted. "It's the most beautiful Christmas tree in the whole world!"

"Let's take a break," Grandma said. "We'll sit on the sofa for a few minutes and admire our work." She found the trailing end of the strings and strings of lights and plugged it into a wall socket. The tree exploded with hundreds of bright pinpoints of colored light.

Maggie sank back on the sofa and sighed happily. "It's gorgeous!"

"Except," Lisa said, "that the lights at the top of the tree twinkle on and off, and the lights at the bottom of the tree don't."

"I know," Grandma said as she settled next to Maggie. "Some of the strands still twinkle, and some don't, and I can never remember which is which. Last year the bottom of the tree twinkled. The year before it was the middle."

Lisa giggled, but Maggie said, "I like it that way."

"It's—uh—original," Lisa said.

Grandma laughed. "It's an interior decorator's nightmare."

"Interior decorators always designed our tree," Maggie said quietly, and added, "when we were home long enough to have a tree."

"You're kidding." Lisa twisted to stare at Maggie. "I didn't know interior decorators designed Christmas trees."

"Last year," Maggie said, "our tree was a pale coral color, decorated with aqua velvet bows, and all the ornaments were crystal. And the year before that—no. That year my father was filming in England, and we didn't have a tree. It was three years ago and the very worst tree I ever saw in my life. It was silver, and the ornaments were weird shapes cut out of black patent leather."

"Yuck!" Lisa said.

"I know, but some crazy people were impressed with that stupid tree. Two magazines and a newspaper sent photographers to take pictures of it." Maggie shivered and wiggled her right hand into Grandma's, comforted by the warm, firm pressure of Grandma's fingers.

"This is my first *real* Christmas tree," she added, "and I'm glad that I'm here with Grandma." She didn't say aloud what she was thinking, that this was going to be a happy Christmas with her aunts and uncles and cousins and her best friend, Lisa, and not the unhappy Christmas she would have had with her father and Kiki.

Maggie loved her father. At least she did when she wasn't angry with him. Sometimes she wondered if they'd ever be able to get along with each other. She constantly seemed to disappoint him. He constantly managed to infuriate her.

Now Roger was married again and didn't need her. That was why he had sent her to live for a summer with Grandma Landry, her mother's mother, and why he hadn't objected when Maggie asked to stay on with her grandmother, going to school in Houston, instead of to another in a long line of boarding schools. Maggie had finally met Roger's wife, Kiki, a twenty-year-old starlet whose visit in Houston had been so short that Maggie really didn't get to know her.

"Kiki has a delightful sense of humor," Grandma had said

to Maggie after Roger and Kiki's brief visit in November. "And she's very friendly. We all had such fun at dinner, helping her celebrate her twenty-first birthday." Grandma had nodded emphatically, as though she had just made up her mind. "Yes. I like Kiki."

But Maggie had just shrugged. Kiki and Roger lived in a different world, a world that Maggie didn't want. Maggie was perfectly content to stay with Grandma in Grandma's world.

"You're daydreaming, Maggie," Lisa said, giving her a poke in her ribs. "Wake up. We're talking about the Christmas cookies."

"The Christmas cookies are supposed to be a secret!" Maggie said. "Why did you tell Grandma?"

"Because we have to bake them somewhere, and while you were off thinking about something else, I voted for your grandmother's kitchen. If we used the kitchen in my house, my little brother and sister would be right in the middle of everything we were doing."

"Grandma," Maggie said seriously, "Lisa and I are going to buy all the ingredients and make thousands—well, hundreds— of cookies and give them as our presents to everyone in our families and to Gloria and to some of our friends. And some will be your present, but now you know about them. I wish you didn't have to know."

"Know what?" Grandma asked.

"About the cookies."

"What cookies? Did someone say 'cookies'? I think I have amnesia."

Maggie jumped to her feet, bouncing with excitement. "This is going to be the most wonderful Christmas ever! Lisa and I are going to put on a special Christmas program, too! We're writing a script for it, and it's funny!"

"Everybody's going to laugh until they get stomachaches," Lisa said.

"We laugh so much while we're writing it that we can't finish it," Maggie said.

"We're going to put the program on here and then do it again at my house for my family."

"Why don't we invite your family over here so we can all watch your program together?" Grandma asked Lisa. "We'll make a real party of it."

"Can Gloria and her children come?" Maggie asked.

"Of course," Grandma said. "And why don't you invite some of your friends from school to come, too?"

"Yeahhh!" Lisa shouted. "It's going to be wild!"

"Lisa," Maggie said, tugging at her friend's arm, "come on. Let's work on our script. If we don't finish writing it pretty soon, it won't be ready in time."

The telephone rang, and Maggie said, "I'll get it." She dashed into the kitchen, grabbed the receiver, and shouted, "Hello!"

The calm, deep voice that answered her was like a cap put on a fizzing bottle of ginger ale. The bubbles inside Maggie were still there. They just weren't shooting up and out. Maggie reached to tug over the nearest chair and sat in it, taking a deep breath to calm down.

"Daddy," she said. "I didn't know it would be you."

"I've got some interesting news for you," Roger said.

"Oh, and I have for you, too," Maggie said. "Lisa and I are writing a program and—"

"Margaret," Roger interrupted. "I have a meeting to go to. I haven't much time."

Maggie could tell that her father was trying to hide the impatience in his voice. *I've done it again,* she thought. "I'm sorry, Daddy," she said, and waited for what he had to tell her.

When he spoke, his voice was deliberately cheerful. "I'm sending you a surprise," he said. "An airline ticket to Los Angeles."

Maggie gasped and gripped the telephone. She tried to speak but couldn't.

"Did you hear me, Margaret?" Roger asked.

Maggie's voice was barely more than a whisper. "For when?"

"For your two-week Christmas vacation," he said. "Kiki and I want you to spend Christmas at the beach house with us."

"But, Daddy," Maggie said, "I can't!" She realized that she was pressing one hand against a sudden pain in her stomach. "Lisa and I are putting on a program, and Grandma promised to have a party for us, and—"

"Margaret, listen to me," Roger said. "I admit that I hadn't taken into consideration that you might have planned some vacation activities with your friends, but I think you'll have to agree with me that being with your parents takes priority."

Maggie's jaw jutted forward. "Kiki is your wife. She's not my parent."

"Don't take that attitude with me, young lady."

"I'm not 'taking an attitude,' Daddy. I'm trying to explain."

"And I'm trying to tell you that I think your Christmas vacation time is a perfect chance for you and Kiki to become better acquainted."

"I've already met her."

"Margaret—"

"Daddy, I can visit you some other time—maybe at spring break."

"I'll begin filming my next picture in February. Right now both Kiki and I are free to entertain you. Later, this spring, we won't be."

"I don't have to be entertained. Honestly! I—oh, Daddy, please! I want to spend Christmas with Grandma!"

"Margaret, I don't think we need to discuss this any further." His voice was cold, and Maggie knew she had hurt him. She hadn't meant to. But didn't he know how he had hurt her, too? "Your ticket has already been mailed to you by air express. It should arrive on Monday. If you have any problems or questions about it, you can call me—or my secretary."

Maggie rubbed at the warm tears that were spilling down her cheeks. "Okay," she managed to say.

"Good-bye, Margaret. We'll see you soon." He paused, and his voice became softer. "I love you."

"Good-bye, Daddy." Maggie hung up quickly. She rested her head and arms on the kitchen table and exploded into tears.

This wasn't going to be the best Christmas vacation she ever had. She was going to be left out of all the fun, so it would be the most miserable and horrible vacation that anyone could imagine!

2

"Roger loves you, Maggie. It's only natural that Christmas wouldn't be happy for him without you," Grandma said.

"That's not why he wants me to come," Maggie grumbled. "He's got some idea that it's a good time for Kiki and me to become better acquainted."

"Perhaps it is," Grandma said.

"Grandma!" Maggie wailed. "Do you want me to go, too?"

Grandma fumbled in the pocket of her slacks for a tissue, then blew her nose. Maggie was astonished to see that her grandmother's eyes were wet. "Of course not!" Grandma said.

Lisa dropped into a kitchen chair across the table from Maggie. "I can't believe it!" She groaned. "What about our cookies and our Christmas program? And the party? Oh, Maggie, I can't stand it!"

"Maybe I just won't go," Maggie said.

Grandma sat up a little straighter and brushed a strand of reddish brown hair back from her eyes. "Why does all the fun have to take place during those two weeks? Why can't it spill over? I have a great idea. We'll make the cookies and have the party and program on the Saturday after Maggie gets back."

Lisa looked dubious. "A Christmas party in January?"

"Why not?" Grandma said. "It can either be the last Christmas party of the season or the first Christmas party of the next season."

Maggie couldn't help smiling. "What about the Christmas tree?"

"We'll keep it up. And we'll open your presents then— unless you can't wait and want to take them with you."

"I'll wait," Maggie said.

"Let's call it The Very First Christmas Party of the Year," Lisa said. "That's almost as funny as our program."

Grandma stood and held out a hand to Maggie. "Why don't you and Lisa get to work on your script right now while I put some chicken in the oven for dinner?" As Maggie got up, Grandma gave her a hug. "Now you'll have two Christmas celebrations," she said.

"Yours will be best," Maggie murmured. "The one with Daddy and Kiki will be boring."

"Maybe not," Lisa said. "Maybe you'll have another patent leather tree."

"I didn't say we had a patent leather *tree!*" But Lisa was giggling, and Maggie had to giggle, too.

"See—it's all going to work out nicely," Grandma said.

But Maggie knew it wouldn't.

Somehow the script for the Christmas program was written, but the jokes didn't seem to be as funny as they had seemed at first. Cookies were baked, but half of the cookie dough was tucked into Grandma's freezer to be taken out for The Very First Christmas Party of the Year. And the last week of school before Christmas vacation passed too quickly.

Before she was really ready, Maggie found herself, tearful and still protesting, on the plane to Los Angeles, California.

Maggie had intended to be cool and calm so that her father would be well aware that she hadn't wanted to come, but when she saw Roger eagerly searching for her among the deplaning passengers, she called out, "Dad!" and ran toward him. Roger met her with a hug, which Maggie eagerly returned. She loved her father. In spite of everything, she really did. With passengers swirling around them like water around rocks in midstream, Maggie and her father stood apart and looked at each other.

"You've grown, Margaret. You're tall for thirteen."

"Daddy, you just saw me last month. I haven't grown since then."

"Well—you're looking very pretty."

"I lost five more pounds."

"Good for you."

"I brought you a Christmas present. I made it myself."

"Fine . . . oh, fine."

"It's for Kiki, too." Maggie stretched, looking to both sides. "Where is Kiki?"

"Kiki didn't come. She thought we'd like a chance to spend some time together, so we could talk."

"What do you want to talk about?"

"Talk about? I don't know, Margaret. Whatever comes to mind. Whatever anyone talks about."

"I'm sorry. I thought you meant something special."

A woman, who was trying to juggle two large shopping bags that were stuffed to overflowing with packages, bumped into Maggie, knocking her off balance.

Roger grabbed Maggie's arm, steadying her. "We're in the way here. Let's get your luggage."

Before long the luggage was stashed in the trunk of Roger's Mercedes, and he and Maggie were on the freeway heading toward the Pacific Coast Highway. "We'll take the scenic route to the Colony," her father said. "It's a little slower, but we're in no hurry."

Maggie decided that grownups really didn't know how to talk to children. No matter how genial and jovial her father tried to sound, they weren't having a conversation. They were engaged in a question-answer game, with Roger asking the questions and Maggie answering them.

"How is school?"

"Fine."

"How is your friend Liza?"

"Her name is *Lisa*, Daddy, and she's fine."

"Are you going to be in any more plays together? Are you having fun? Why don't you tell me about the interesting things that you and Lisa are doing?"

Maggie didn't want to talk about their Christmas plans. It hurt too much that they had been spoiled. But her father was waiting, expecting her to say something, so as they turned onto the highway that snaked along the edge of the deep blue Pacific Ocean, she turned her attention from the palm trees and the sparklets of sun on the water and reluctantly told him about The Very First Christmas Party of the Year.

"Cute idea," he said.

And the script that she and Lisa had written.

"Houston's answer to New York and Hollywood," he said.

And Grandma's wonderful Christmas tree.

Roger said, "I wonder if Kiki's remembered to hire someone to do a tree for us."

Maggie shifted to face her father. "Couldn't we decorate a tree ourselves? Couldn't we have a tree like Grandma's?"

"It would take a lot of work and trouble."

"Didn't you ever have a tree like that when you were a boy? Didn't you decorate it with your family?"

For a few moments Roger concentrated on changing lanes. Finally he answered, "My parents didn't have much money. Our Christmas trees were pretty skimpy."

"Then now's your chance to have a really fun Christmas tree." She leaned forward eagerly, waiting for his decision.

Finally her father said, "We'll leave the choice up to Kiki."

The beach house hadn't changed. Gleaming white and crowded against its equally expensive neighbors, it opened wide glass eyes to the sea. The huge living room held low sofas bunched with bright pillows. Larger versions of the pillows were piled on the wide outside deck.

As Roger and Maggie stepped onto the deck that faced the ocean, Kiki waved and called to them. She ran up from the sand, her blond hair blowing around her face and into her mouth. She was barefooted and looked tanned in her white shorts and blouse, and she hugged Maggie with delight.

"I'm so glad you're here! I'm so glad!" She laughed as she tried to pull an unruly strand of hair from her mouth.

Maggie stiffened. Kiki behaved as though they were good friends, and they weren't. But Kiki didn't seem to notice Maggie's aloofness. She followed Maggie to the room that had always been Maggie's and flopped onto the bed.

"Want me to help you unpack?" she asked.

Maggie began pulling things from her suitcase and stuffing them into the open bureau drawers. "No, thanks," she said. "I haven't got much to unpack. I traveled light because I'll be going home—back to Grandma's—soon."

"That's smart," Kiki said. "If I had my way, I'd just wear shorts and blouses all the time."

She sat up as Maggie hung up the two dresses she had

brought with her and tucked her suitcase into the closet. "I hope you have a good time here, Margaret."

"It's Maggie. I like to be called *Maggie*. I was named after Grandma, and everybody calls her *Maggie*, so I want to be Maggie, too."

"Okay, Maggie." Kiki leaned forward. "I know you're going to miss your grandmother and all the Christmas season fun she was planning. I know it was hard for you to come here at this time."

Maggie stared at her. "Do you really know?"

"Trust me," Kiki said. "I know. But I also know how much your father loves you and misses you."

Maggie just shrugged.

She expected Kiki to say more about her father, maybe even give her the kind of short lecture that grownups think they have to give in sticky situations. But Kiki didn't. She hopped off the bed and said, "What would you like to do while you're here? What would make you the very happiest?"

That's when Maggie told her about Grandma's tree.

"Oh, yes!" Kiki clasped her hands together. "With angels and Santa Clauses and candy canes! Let's go tell Roger." She grabbed one of Maggie's hands and ran into the living room. "Roger!" she cried. "We're going to have the most wonderful Christmas tree! Come with us! We're going to buy ornaments! And a tree!"

"Right now?" Roger asked. He looked startled.

"Yes! Right now," Kiki said.

"We can't," Roger said. He looked at his watch. "Mrs. Blake has planned a little party this afternoon for Maggie."

"Oh, dear. I forgot," Kiki said.

"I don't know any Mrs. Blake," Maggie told her father. "Why do I have to go to her party?"

Roger spoke slowly and distinctly in his I'm-trying-to-bepatient tone of voice. "Mrs. Blake lives next door," he said. "Her son is Timmy Blake. I'm sure you've seen the television series in which he stars."

"Timmy is your age, Maggie," Kiki broke in.

"I know who he is," Maggie said. "He looks conceited."

"Margaret," Roger said, "I think it was very kind of Mrs. Blake to plan this party so that you'll meet other young people."

"I don't want to meet other young people," Maggie said. She knew she was being difficult, but she didn't care. No one had asked her if she wanted to go to a party with strangers. It was bad enough having to be here in Malibu instead of in Houston with Grandma. Somebody should have asked her what she wanted to do instead of planning everything for her.

"It doesn't matter whether you want to go or not," Roger announced. "The party starts in an hour, so I'd suggest that you change to an appropriate dress and comb your hair so that you'll look presentable."

Maggie's eyes burned with the tears she forced back. She wouldn't let her father see how much he had hurt her. He'd never change, and she wouldn't change. Her two weeks in Malibu would be just as unhappy as she had thought they would be. Maggie whirled and ran back into the bedroom, slamming the door behind her.

3

A few minutes later Maggie heard a light tap on her bedroom door.

"I'm getting dressed, Daddy. Don't come in," Maggie called.

"It's me—Kiki. May I come in?"

Maggie took a deep breath to steady herself. She hoped that the cold water she had splashed on her face had taken away the blotchy redness around her eyes. "Sure."

Kiki slipped through the door, closing it softly behind her. "I'm sorry I forgot about that party," she said.

"It's not your fault." Maggie shrugged.

"You don't have to wear a dress," Kiki said. "Roger thought it was going to be one of those dressy things, but I found out from Nora Blake that it's casual. The caterer's going to barbecue chicken or something out on their patio. So wear shorts, if you'd like, or a skirt and blouse. Even jeans."

Maggie sat on the edge of the bed. "I won't know anyone there."

"You'll know me," Kiki said, "and Roger."

"I thought the party was for kids."

"Kids and their parents."

"I'm glad I won't be there by myself."

"I used to hate meeting new people," Kiki said. "I always wanted to sit under the stairs and hide."

"You? But you're so friendly with everyone."

"I had to learn to be," Kiki said. "It was hard."

Maggie sighed. "I guess that I shouldn't have got so mad at Daddy. We always say the wrong things to each other. We can't seem to get along."

"Probably because you're so much alike," Kiki said.

Maggie bristled. "I'm not anything like Daddy. I'm like my mother. I even look just like my mother."

"She must have been very beautiful," Kiki said.

Maggie opened her mouth in surprise, then closed it again. "I wish I could remember her," she said more calmly. "I wish I knew if we thought about things in the same way."

Kiki put a hand on Maggie's shoulder. "I'd better get ready for the party myself." She paused at the doorway. "One thing about Hollywood parties—at least the food's always good."

"What's Timmy Blake like?"

Kiki shrugged. "You'll have to find that out for yourself."

Maggie was familiar with the television series that had made Timmy Blake a star. Timmy played the part of Dick Dackery, who flew via spaceship with his father, private detective Doc Dackery, and solved crimes in outer space. He had sun-bleached blond hair and blue eyes, which matched his blue spacesuit. A lot of the girls at school never missed the Wednesday night program because of Timmy. Lisa was one of them. Maggie smiled to herself as she thought what fun it would be to tell Lisa about meeting Timmy Blake. Lisa would die. Maybe she could bring Lisa Timmy's autograph.

But she changed her mind when she met Timmy. "So glad

you could come," he said to Maggie. He was handsome and charming and friendly, but she felt as though she had been greeted by a robot. His eyes were screens, and the real Timmy was hiding somewhere behind them.

He shook hands with Roger and Kiki while Timmy's plump mother wrapped her arms around Maggie and gushed. "Isn't she adorable! What a darling! What a treasure you have here, Roger!"

Maggie felt herself blushing. It was bad enough to have Mrs. Blake gurgling in her ear, but other guests at the party had turned to look at her.

"Timmy, dear," Mrs. Blake said loudly, "why don't you take Margaret out to the deck? Dinner's not ready yet, but we have all sorts of soft drinks out there in a bucket of ice."

"Good idea," Timmy said heartily. As some of the other guests stepped forward to say hello to her father and Kiki, Maggie allowed herself to be led through the crowd out to the deck.

As they went through the sliding glass doors, closing them behind them, Timmy let go of Maggie's hand. "What do you want to drink?" he asked disinterestedly.

"I don't care. Anything," she said.

"Help yourself," he said, leaning against the glass. "They're all in the bucket of ice over there."

The spacious deck was covered with small round tables and chairs. Each table was colorful with red and pink napkins, pots of red poinsettias, and small gift boxes tied in silver ribbon. Large bunches of red and pink balloons were tied to the deck railing, and they bobbed and bounced in the breeze. At one end of the deck a large, stuffed plastic Santa Claus held his arms out wide, and at the other end a grill had been set up, where a man dressed in a chef's spotless white coat and hat was barbecuing various kinds of meat. Beyond the deck a strip of glistening sand met a gold-brushed ocean.

"My father said there would be a lot of kids here," Maggie told Timmy.

"We don't know a lot of kids," he answered. "Anyhow, my mother would never ask anyone my age to come to a party to which producers and directors are invited."

"Why not?"

"Competition. Rule number one. You never give the competition a chance to make points."

"I don't understand you," Maggie said. "This is supposed to be a party, isn't it? You make it sound like an audition."

"That's what parties are for," he said. "Before this party is over, my mother will be talking to your father about a part that is coming up in the next film he's going to make. She wants me to have a shot at it."

"And you don't want her to. Right?"

"It doesn't matter. It's my job."

Maggie took a can of root beer and popped the top open. This conversation was making her uncomfortable, and she wanted to change the subject. "Your decorations are very— uh—interesting," she said.

"Interesting?" He laughed. "My mother wouldn't appreciate that description. I think her word for all this was 'stunning.' So was her party decorator's."

"At least it's not silver and black patent leather," Maggie said, and she told him about her father's famous Christmas tree.

"If it got him press coverage, don't knock it," Timmy said.

Maggie would have liked to dump her root beer on Timmy's boring head. Instead she quickly said, "I think I'll go walk on the beach for a while."

"Okay. Whatever you want." Timmy took a few steps toward the stairs that led down to the sand.

"By myself," Maggie said firmly.

"But I'm supposed to entertain you."

"Why? I can't do anything for you."

For the first time Timmy looked right at her and seemed to come to life. "Hey, don't get mad. I didn't mean it the way it sounded. I just meant that I was the host, and I wanted you to have a good time."

"I'm not having a good time," Maggie said. "I didn't want to come to your party in the first place. I don't want to be here any more than you do."

Timmy's grin was so wicked that it reminded Maggie of her friend Jerico. "Then let's both cut out," he said. "We won't have to be polite and talk to all those people in there. We can take some food with us and go farther down the beach. How about it?"

"Well," Maggie said reluctantly, "if you want to."

"I really do want to," he said. "Come on. Let's see if any of that chicken is cooked. If it isn't, there's all sorts of salads and stuff that we can take."

But some of the chicken was ready, so they heaped their plates high with samples from all the dishes and carried them down the stairs.

"Where to?" Timmy asked.

"Not too far," Maggie said as she tried to juggle her plate and soft-drink can. "I don't want to spill this."

"Let's sit on the stairs to your deck," Timmy suggested. "They're on the opposite side, and no one will even see us there. We can relax in privacy."

"Okay," Maggie said, and she trudged through the sand without mishap, gingerly sitting on the bottom stair and lowering the wobbly plate to her lap.

For a few moments they ate hungrily, not bothering to talk, then Maggie sighed happily and said, "This is good, Timmy."

"Don't call me Timmy," he said. "I hate it. Timmy is a

name for someone under the age of five. Call me Blake. That's what my father—my father on the show, that is—calls me. Pete calls me Blake."

"Peter Harding. What's he like?"

Blake perked up. "He's great. He had a basketball hoop put up on the lot. Sometimes we shoot a few baskets together. Once he took me to a Rams game." He paused, picking up a drumstick and putting it back onto his plate. "I wish Pete could have come to the party today, but he's spending the holidays in Acapulco."

Maggie took a last swallow of her root beer and put the can on the steps with her nearly empty plate. "All right. From now on I'll call you Blake, and you can call me Maggie," she said. "I don't think of myself as a Margaret anymore."

"Tell me what you like to do," Blake said. "Are you at all interested in acting?"

Maggie told him about her role in the high school play and about the trick Jerico and Carter played on her during the junior-high review.

Blake grinned. "Some of the adults have pulled some wild stuff on the set," he said, "but the kids wouldn't dare. They'd really be in trouble. Any delay costs money."

Maggie leaned back against the railing and sighed. "You've got a one-track mind," she said. "I don't think you can talk about anything but television and movies."

Blake was silent for a few moments. Then he said, "I guess you're right, but it's because that's all I know. I've been acting since I was six months old and made my debut on the 'All Our Boys' situation comedy."

"Do you like being a famous actor?" Maggie asked.

"I guess."

"What's it like when you go to Baskin-Robbins for ice cream and people rush up to get your autograph?"

"I don't. I can't go to places like Baskin-Robbins because that's exactly what people do. It isn't safe."

"You mean you can't just go to the movies when you feel like it, or out for a hamburger, or shopping in the mall?"

"No," Blake said. "I can't."

"That's horrible!" Maggie said.

"No, it's not," he told her. "I make enough money so that my mother and I can have just about anything we want."

"Except freedom."

"Freedom?"

He looked so puzzled that Maggie hurried to change the subject. "I suppose sometimes it could be fun having other kids recognize you as Dick Dackery."

"Sure," he said. "The personal appearances are fun."

This time it was Maggie's turn to look confused, so Blake said, "I'm doing a personal appearance tomorrow at the Westside Children's Hospital. I'll visit the children along with Santa Claus, and some elves will be there to hand out presents. Want to come with me?"

"Well—" Maggie hesitated.

"I wish you would," Blake said.

"Okay," Maggie said. "If it's all right with your mother and my father."

"There's no reason why it wouldn't be—" Blake began, but he was interrupted by voices yelling from the direction of his house.

"Timmy! Margaret!" A woman was screaming.

Deeper voices came closer. "Don't panic!" a man was saying. "They must be all right!"

Roger Ledoux ran around the corner of their house, coming to a stumbling halt as he faced Maggie. He turned and waved toward Blake's house, yelling to someone, "They're here!" But as Roger turned back to Maggie, his eyes sparked with anger. "What do you mean running off like that?" he snapped.

"We didn't run off," Maggie said. "Well, we did, but—"

"Didn't it occur to you that Mrs. Blake would be frantic? She was terrified that the two of you had been kidnapped!"

Blake spoke up. "It wasn't Maggie's fault. I suggested that we find a quiet place over here to eat."

Maggie opened her mouth, trying to find the right words to share the blame, but Blake, once more as poised and charming as he appeared to be on television, draped an arm around Maggie's shoulders and smiled at Roger. "We can't blame Maggie," he added. "She isn't used to the special problems of the film world."

Before Roger could answer, Blake said, "I have to make a hospital appearance tomorrow morning as Dick Dackery. I asked Maggie to go with me, but naturally she said she'd have to get your permission. Is it okay with you, Mr. Ledoux? We'll take good care of her."

"Why—uh—yes, if she'd like to." Roger blinked.

Blake picked up his paper plate and Maggie's, too. "We'd better not stay here and chat," he said. "It's time to get back to the party and make Mom happy."

Blake strode on ahead, whistling, while Maggie fell into step with her father. "We were just looking for a place to sit down," she said. "We didn't know his mother would get so excited."

"After this, don't wander off," Roger said. "Stay near adult supervision. Right now Timmy's a hot property."

Maggie stopped so suddenly that she kicked up a ruff of fine sand. "He's a person, Daddy! Not a 'property'! "

"Of course he's a person," her father said. "I simply meant that he's in the public eye, and because of that he can attract people who can be a nuisance—even dangerous."

"Then why does anyone want to get to be famous?"

"You wouldn't understand," Roger said, and led the way up the steps to the Blakes' outer deck, where a wave of laughter and music had washed away everyone's earlier fears.

"I asked the wrong person," Maggie mumbled to herself, and wished she could talk about Timmy Blake with Grandma.

The only other "young people" invited to Mrs. Blake's party were a seven-year-old television actress, who had a practically toothless grin and who complained to everyone she met that she had to wear false teeth on the set until her own permanent teeth grew in, and her eight-year-old brother, who plopped in front of the TV and refused to talk to anybody.

Blake's mother, with a tight grip around his shoulders and a smile so wide that it stretched her face, led him from one conversation group to another, where he smiled and chatted with the other adults.

The seven-year-old tugged on Maggie's arm. "Are you anybody?" she asked.

"Shhhh," Maggie answered. "Don't blow my cover. I'm here in disguise." She walked out to the deck, elbowing her way between the guests and tables. The musicians had taken a break, leaving their instruments propped against the deck rail. Maggie edged around a guitar, leaned on the rail, and watched the waves rhythmically heave upward, then smack the damp sand, fizzling out with a poof of foam. Like this party. A real fizzle. She could hardly wait for the wonderful party she and Lisa were going to have, The Very First Christmas Party of the Year.

Someone stepped up beside her and picked up the guitar. "Hi," Kiki said brightly. "Having fun?"

"With all the young people?" Maggie snapped. She took a deep breath and said, "I'm sorry. I didn't mean to be rude."

Kiki lightly strummed a few chords as she answered, "Maybe Timmy's friends are out of town for the holidays."

"I don't think he has many friends," Maggie said. "And he doesn't like to be called 'Timmy.' He told me to call him 'Blake.' "

"Thanks for the tip," Kiki murmured. She fingered the guitar in a rippling scale and grinned. "Want to liven up this party?"

"How?" Maggie asked.

"Just hang on and follow me," Kiki answered. She began to play the guitar loudly and sing as she wound her way between the tables.

Maggie shyly did as Kiki asked, hoping that no one would stare at her. No one took time to stare. They hopped up and got in line, some of them singing along with Kiki. Someone held Maggie's waist, just as she was holding Kiki's. Many of the guests inside the house ran out to get in line, too. Kiki laughed and led the line down the stairs to the sand, where they snaked back and forth, singing and laughing, until Kiki finally plopped down on the sand.

Following her lead, they sat around her. Kiki began another song, one that everyone seemed to know, and they sang with her. This time Maggie sang. She knew all the words to this song.

Blake squeezed in next to her, singing in a clear, strong

voice. *He does have a nice smile,* Maggie thought and smiled back. She thought about his invitation to go with him tomorrow to visit the children in the hospital. Maybe she'd go; maybe she wouldn't. She hadn't decided yet. It might be fun to see Blake in costume as Dick Dackery. She wondered if he ever got confused as to which part of him was Dackery and which part was Blake. Sometimes he seemed to be one and sometimes the other. Yes. She'd tell him later. She would go.

When Blake and his mother picked Maggie up the next morning in a long black car with dark tinted windows, he was dressed in his blue spacesuit, complete with helmet. They sat in the backseat while Mrs. Blake drove. Maggie tried to think of something to say, but she only giggled.

"What's so funny?" Blake asked.

"I feel as though you've just dropped in from outer space," Maggie said. "Maybe it's the helmet."

Blake took it off, scowling at it. "I thought you'd want to see the whole outfit."

"I have," Maggie said. "Every Wednesday night on television."

Blake perked up. "You watch my show?"

"Of course. Everybody I know does."

He relaxed against the seat, smiling contentedly, and Maggie was glad that for once she had said the right thing.

All the way to the Westside Children's Hospital Mrs. Blake chatted about Blake's career, hardly giving Maggie or Blake a chance to speak. Maggie was glad when they arrived and a committee rushed to the car to escort them into the hospital lobby.

Maggie was no sooner inside the door when a woman grabbed her arm and tugged her into a nearby room. "You're late," the woman said, holding out what looked like a bright green leotard. "Here. All the other elves are dressed. Get into your costume."

"I'm not an elf," Maggie told her. "I just came with Blake—uh—Timmy Blake."

"Oh, dear," the woman said. "We're short one elf." She held the garment up to Maggie. "You'd fit into this. Do you want to be an elf and help give out the presents?"

"Sure," Maggie said. "Why not?"

"Oh—one question," the woman said. "Are you SAG or not?"

"I don't know what you mean," Maggie said.

"It's your status as an actress," the woman said. "We can't pay scale. That's why if you're SAG, I can't use you."

Maggie was still confused. "If I were SAG, someone would have told me by this time," she said. "What are the symptoms?"

The woman sighed. "Apparently you don't know that professional actors belong to Screen Actors Guild and must be paid by union-scale rules. That's what SAG means."

"You don't have to pay me," Maggie said.

"Oh, yes," the woman said. "Our Women's Guild will mail checks for twenty-five dollars to all the elves' agents. In your case we'll mail the check directly to you. Give me your name and address." She scribbled them quickly on a note pad and shoved the costume at Maggie.

"But isn't Timmy Blake a member of SAG?" Maggie asked.

"Timmy is a volunteer."

"Let me be a volunteer, too," Maggie said, but the woman had rushed through the door, shutting it firmly behind her. Maggie liked the fact that Blake had volunteered his time to visit the children. When he wasn't pretending to be Dick Dackery, Blake was kind of nice.

As Maggie finished putting on her costume, a fellow elf suddenly appeared. She was short and thin with brown hair curling from under her pointed cap and looked close to Maggie's age. "Hi," she said. "They told me to get you. Are you ready?"

"I don't know." Maggie giggled. "Do I look like an elf?"

"As much as I do." The girl laughed. "My name is Truly Norris. What's yours?"

"Maggie Ledoux."

"Let's go, Maggie."

Maggie put a hand on Truly's arm to stop her. "Wait a minute. What are we supposed to do?"

"You should have come to rehearsal. We're supposed to follow Santa and Timmy Blake and hand out presents and act like—well—the way elves act."

The woman who had led Maggie to this room poked her head through the open doorway. "Will you two please hurry!"

"We're ready," Maggie said, and she raced to the door with Truly.

There were six other elves, and they were herded into a cluster behind Blake and a very fat Santa who grumbled, "Move it, kids. I haven't got all day."

"Bah, humbug," Maggie whispered to Truly, who clapped a hand over her mouth to keep from laughing.

"Down the hall and turn to the right," the woman leader ordered. The pack moved ahead.

"I haven't seen you at any of the auditions," Truly whispered to Maggie. "Are you new in town?"

"I'm not an actress," Maggie whispered back. "I just tagged along with Timmy Blake, and they were short one elf, so I agreed to fill in."

"You know Timmy Blake?" Truly's eyes widened.

Maggie nodded. "If you want to meet him, I'll introduce you after this is over."

"Oh, I do!" Truly said. As they reached the door to one of the wings, she added, "Someday I'm going to be a famous star, just like he is. Someday."

"Hush!" the woman said, glaring at Maggie and Truly. Rushing as though she were late for a plane, she shoved bulging, brown canvas sacks at each of the elves.

"Let's get this show on the road," Santa snapped. "I've got other things to do."

Blake drew his shiny supersonic space dissolver from the holster at his hip and poked the end of it into Santa's pillowed stomach. "Lighten up, Santa," he said with Dick Dackery firmness. "We're going to put on a good show for these kids, no matter how long it takes. We can always shrink you to two inches and bring in another Santa—one who wants to give these kids a good show."

"Okay, okay," Santa said quickly. "Big smile. See?" He pushed open the door and entered the large room shouting, "Ho, ho, ho!"

Blake turned and winked at Maggie, "And a ha, ha, ha," he whispered.

Yes, Maggie decided. She liked Timmy Blake very much.

5

Some of the children were in wheelchairs. Most were propped up in beds, and a number of them wore plaster casts or bandages. A few looked ready to bounce out of bed. Others appeared pale and tired. But as Santa Claus and Dick Dackery made their way through the room, stopping to talk to each child, it seemed to Maggie as though someone had flipped a switch to turn extra lights on smiling lips and shining eyes. There were giggles and laughter, shrieks of joy, and cries of "Santa Claus! Come over here! Don't forget me!"

Maggie, Truly, and the other elves scurried about, handing out gifts, which the children eagerly clutched. But Maggie could see that Dick Dackery outshone even the gifts and Santa Claus. He was someone the children knew as a friend, someone who came into their lives every Wednesday evening, and they were all eager to touch him and talk to him.

Blake did a great job of giving them what they wanted. He picked up some of the little ones, shook hands with the older ones, and behaved as though he had all the time in the world to spend with them.

They had so many questions. "What's it like in outer space?"

"Were you scared when the space pirates were chasing you?"

"Does your father let you help fly the spaceship?"

"Can you bring a Worple back to our planet?"

Blake answered all the questions seriously, as Dick Dackery would, until the woman with the Guild announced through . her smile that Santa and Dick Dackery *must* hurry on to meet more of the children. With nervous flutters she shooed them from the ward, replenished the elves' sacks, and herded them into the next wing of the hospital to repeat their performances.

By noon all of the children had been visited, the elves' costumes had been collected, and the performers and their parents were led into a room next to the hospital cafeteria for soft drinks and hamburgers.

Truly tugged a long, thin man over to meet Maggie. "This is my father," she said.

He greeted Maggie solemnly. She was uncomfortable, knowing he was appraising her.

"Maggie doesn't want to be an actress," Truly said. "She came because she's Timmy Blake's friend."

Mr. Norris's eyebrows shot up like two fuzzy caterpillars standing on end. He immediately became more interested in Maggie. "Have you known him long?" he asked.

"He lives next door," Maggie said.

"In the Colony?" Mr. Norris asked, although he apparently already knew Blake's address.

"Yes," Maggie answered.

"Ledoux. Ledoux," Mr. Norris mumbled to himself, scowling as he tried to place the name.

Maggie hoped he wouldn't. She was glad when Truly grabbed her arm and said, "Let's get something to eat. Look, some of the others have already started."

Maggie took her hamburger and drink from the guild woman and sat at a nearby table, next to Truly. Maggie raised her hamburger to take a bite, but stopped as a hand gripped her shoulder.

"Be polite. Wait for me," Blake said, and dropped into the chair on Maggie's right.

Maggie heard Truly gasp and saw that Truly was just as excited to be this close to Blake as the hospitalized children had been. She introduced them.

"Hi," Blake said around a mouthful of hamburger.

"Hi," Truly murmured.

"You were great with the kids," Maggie said to Blake. "They loved you."

He shrugged. "They love Dick Dackery."

"But you *are* Dick Dackery," Truly said.

"Dick Dackery is only make-believe," Blake said. He chomped into his hamburger as though he were getting even with it.

Maggie felt sorry for Blake. Instead of feeling good about making the kids happy, he seemed almost depressed. "You're the one who made Dick Dackery come alive," she told him. "Dick Dackery would be nothing without you."

Blake sat up straighter and blinked as he looked at Maggie. "Yeah?" He nodded. "I hadn't thought about that."

"Didn't your drama teacher ever tell you how the actor makes the character?"

"I never had a drama teacher," Blake said. "I've been acting since before I can remember, since I was a baby."

"Then how did you learn what to do?"

He looked surprised. "The director always tells me." He paused and added, "And my father—uh, not my real father, because I never see him—I mean Pete. You know—he plays Doc Dackery, my father on the show. He told me I have a natural talent."

"Me, too," Truly said. "That's what my agent told me."

"Who's your agent?" Blake asked.

"Jerry Klinke."

"Never heard of him."

"Oh."

Truly looked so distressed that Maggie turned to Blake and asked, "Now who's being rude?"

"Sorry," Blake mumbled in Truly's direction.

"He's supposed to be a great agent," Truly said eagerly. "We saw his ad in a magazine. My father said that everything in the ad sounded right."

Maggie tried to change the subject. "Does your father always come with you when you're acting?"

Truly nodded. "That's because my father is out of work. My mother works in a bank, so he comes with me instead of my mother. My father tells me that he'll help me to get to be a successful actress in any way he can."

"Does your father want you to be an actress, or do you want to be?" Maggie asked.

"Oh, I do!" Truly quickly answered. "I want to be an actress more than anything in the world!"

Blake stuffed the last bite of hamburger into his mouth and stood up. "Ready to go home?" he asked Maggie.

Maggie nodded.

"I hope I get to see you again," Truly said to Maggie.

Maggie had a sudden idea. "How would you like to help decorate our Christmas tree?"

"When?"

"This afternoon. My stepmother said that this afternoon we could get the tree and the ornaments and decorate it." Maggie couldn't help giving a little bounce. "We're going to get all sorts of ornaments and lights and glittery strands and hang them all over the tree until it looks like my grandmother's Christmas tree!"

Blake looked interested. "That sounds like fun."

"You're invited, too," Maggie said.

"I couldn't go to the store with you to get the ornaments," Blake said.

"Sure you can," Maggie said. "If you're worried about people recognizing you, we'll disguise you."

Blake laughed. "I've never tried that before."

"Come on," Maggie said. She tugged at Truly's hand, pulling her over to where Mr. Norris was leaning against the wall, waiting for his daughter. Maggie told him what she had told Truly, adding, "She can ride back with us, and you can pick her up this evening. I'll give you our address. Will you let her come?"

Mr. Norris nodded and smiled so brightly that Maggie knew he had figured out whose daughter she was. She wished he hadn't. "Thanks for the invitation. Truly will like that," Mr. Norris said and added, "Now, you be a good girl, Truly."

The two girls followed Blake and his mother to their car, Truly muttering, "Why do parents always say that?"

"Because if they forget, even once," Maggie said, "there is no telling what horrible things we might do."

"In your case," Blake said, "I believe it."

"Timmy!" his mother said, looking as shocked as though he had dangled a snake in her face, "What a dreadful thing to say to a sweet girl like Margaret."

"He was just kidding, Mrs. Blake," Maggie said. "He was being funny."

Mrs. Blake shook her head as she climbed into the car and started the ignition. She said firmly, "I don't think remarks like that are humorous."

Maggie scooted over on the backseat next to Truly, and Blake climbed in next to her. She winked at him, thinking how difficult it would be to have a mother without a sense of humor.

But apparently Blake was used to it. As his mother began the drive back to the Malibu Colony, he eagerly told her about their plans to buy ornaments and trim the Ledoux Christmas tree.

"You may help to trim the tree," she said, "but the trip to the store is out. Just think what would happen if you were recognized!"

"We'll disguise him," Maggie said.

"We can't take the chance," Mrs. Blake said. "No. I'm sorry, Margaret, but I can't permit it."

Maggie expected Blake to try to convince his mother, but he just sat quietly and looked out the window as though he were more interested in the houses they were passing than in their conversation.

Mrs. Blake turned her interest to Truly, firing one question after another until Truly mentioned the name of her agent. "Hmmmm," Mrs. Blake murmured, sounding like a cat being tickled behind the ears.

Why this reaction to Truly's agent? Maggie didn't have time to think about it because at that point Mrs. Blake pulled off the highway and turned into Webb Way, the road leading to the Colony. She waved at the gate attendant as she drove past and pulled to a stop in front of the Ledoux house.

Maggie and Truly hopped out of the car, thanking Mrs. Blake.

"Give me a call when you get back from the store," Blake said. "I'll come right over."

"Okay," Maggie said. "If Kiki doesn't have popcorn, we'll get some of that, too."

Mrs. Blake drove off as Truly, eyes wide, stared at the Ledoux house. "Your house is right on the ocean!" she said.

"You can see the ocean from most of the rooms," Maggie told her. "Come on inside."

"Someday I'm going to have a house like this," Truly said.

"You're making a good start," Maggie said. "You're twelve or thirteen—"

"Twelve."

"Twelve, and you're already earning money. Like today."

"No, we didn't get paid today," Truly said. "Mr. Klinke said I was lucky to get this assignment just for the experience."

"But the elves were supposed to be paid."

"No," Truly said. "You're mistaken. If that hospital Women's Guild was going to pay anything, Mr. Klinke would have said so."

Maggie was puzzled. The woman from the guild had talked about twenty-five dollars' payment. Maybe Mr. Klinke didn't know about that. Maybe he and Truly would get a happy surprise when the check came. Or maybe there was something wrong with the way Mr. Klinke did business. "Have you gone on other assignments just for the experience?" Maggie asked Truly.

Truly sighed. "Three of them. In fact, that's all I've done so far. But one of these days I'll get a paying job."

Kiki threw open the front door. "There you are!" she said, and smiled at Truly. "Who's your friend, Maggie?"

Maggie hurried to introduce them, adding, "I invited Truly to help us trim our Christmas tree."

Kiki pulled her car keys from the pocket of her jeans and jangled them in front of Maggie. "Then let's get with it!" she said. "I'll drive."

Maggie paused as Kiki headed toward the door to the garage. "What about Dad? Doesn't he want to come with us?"

"Something came up," Kiki said. "An investor on the next

film is in town today and wanted to discuss it, so Roger didn't have a choice. He had to meet him."

"Will he be back in time to help trim the tree?"

"There's no telling."

"Rats!" Maggie grumbled.

"Hey, look," Kiki said, "we'll make the best of it. Okay? If he's here it will be great, but if he's not, think how much fun you and Truly and I will have in surprising him."

"And Blake," Maggie said. "His mother was afraid to let him go shopping with us, but he wants to come over to help trim the tree."

"We could have disguised him," Kiki said.

"That's just what Maggie wanted to do!" Truly said.

"He could have worn my red wig," Kiki said.

"And a Groucho nose and glasses!"

"And Dad's overcoat!"

They laughed all the way to the garage, where they piled into Kiki's red sports car, and Maggie found herself once more excited about decorating the tree.

The first stop was at a shop in the mall on Ocean Boulevard in Santa Monica, where they bought boxes and boxes of ornaments. Truly liked the colored glass balls, and Maggie carefully chose an assortment of the blown-glass birds and Santas. But Kiki snatched up armfuls of gold and silver tinsel, felt angels with embroidered faces, twinkle lights, painted wooden horses, glass bells, and rainbow-hued metallic icicles.

"This is going to be a tree we'll never forget!" Kiki announced.

Soon the trunk was loaded with their purchases. "Now to buy the tree," Maggie said.

They looked at each other. "The trunk's full. How will we ever fit a tree in the car, too?" Truly said.

"I don't know," Kiki said, "but let's not worry about it. There's a big Christmas tree lot on the next street. If they sell us a tree, it will be up to them to figure out how we'll get it home."

"I like the way you think," Maggie said with a giggle. She stopped laughing and looked at Kiki seriously. "I guess I really do," she added. "I can see why Dad—"

Kiki was waiting for her to finish the sentence, but Maggie suddenly became shy. "Blake will be waiting for us," she said quickly. She ducked her head and climbed into the car.

They found the perfect tree, and somehow Kiki convinced one of the high school boys who worked on the lot that he should load the tree into his pickup truck and follow them up the Pacific Coast Highway to their home in the Colony. Then it was just a matter of telephoning Blake, who arrived almost as soon as Maggie had hung up the receiver.

Together they managed to fit the tree into its stand and string the lights around it. Then each of them began hanging ornaments, often having to climb around or under one of the others in order to reach one of the branches.

Finally, as Maggie and Truly were attaching the last few ornaments, Blake sank back onto one of the sofas and said, "That is the craziest tree I've ever seen."

"What do you mean, crazy?" Maggie stepped back and studied the tree. "It's beautiful, not crazy."

Blake pointed at the tree. "There are too many red balls on that side, and over there it's so crowded that the pink angel looks like she's riding the rocking horse, and there's too much tinsel on that branch at the bottom, and—"

Maggie picked up a small pillow from the nearest chair and threw it at him.

"The tree is perfect," she said. "No more comments."

Kiki smiled. She stepped back and rubbed her hands on the seat of her jeans. "It looks just the way it's supposed to look. At least I think it does. Is it like your grandmother's tree, Maggie?"

"Almost," Maggie said, "except for the stories. Grandma

has a story to go with each ornament, like a funny place where she found it, or when one of her children made it for her at school, or how a friend brought it from another country. Stories like that." She plopped onto the sofa next to Blake.

Truly and Kiki joined them.

A voice spoke from behind them. "Then I'd better tell you the truth about that star at the top of the tree."

Maggie jumped. "Daddy! We didn't hear you come in!"

Roger leaned over and kissed her forehead, kissed Kiki, and was introduced to Truly. He sat in a nearby chair. "It's strange that you should ask about that ornament," he said. "Years ago it was discovered packed in the sea chest of a pirate who was captured down in the Caribbean. It was smuggled into this country and passed from hand to hand. Two months ago the owner, desperately afraid it would be stolen by ruffians who had been slipping threatening notes into her mailbox, frantically looked for a place in which to hide it."

He paused, and Truly bounced up and down. "Who'd think of looking for it in a store that sold Christmas ornaments? Right?"

"Right," Roger said. "But keep it quiet. We don't want to find threatening notes in our mailbox."

Maggie grinned at her father. She hadn't known he could make up stories like that. Or had she? Way back in her mind there was a wiggling memory of his lap before bedtime and stories he had told just to her.

"Those red balls," Blake said, glancing pointedly at Maggie as he added, "the ones that are bunched too close together at the side of the tree—I brought those from outer space. They look good right now, but they're likely to disintegrate at any moment."

"See that angel with the blue lace ruffle?" Truly asked. "That once belonged to the Queen of England."

"Which queen?" Blake interrupted.

"Ummm, well, oh, who cares?" Truly said. "She lived hundreds of years ago, so nobody remembers her name now anyway."

"It's an antique," Maggie said.

"Right. And the queen was very fond of it," Truly added.

Kiki smiled. "I'm fond of the entire tree," she said, "because it's here through the efforts of two elves and a private investigator from outer space."

"That sounds even funnier than the made-up stories, and it's true!" Maggie laughed.

"We forgot the popcorn," Blake said.

"I don't think that tree would hold another thing," Roger told him.

"Not for the tree—for us!" Blake answered. "I'm getting hungry."

"How about hot dogs?" Kiki asked as she scrambled to her feet. "I'll make them while you three tell Roger about the hospital visit."

So they did.

"The woman in charge told me that Blake had volunteered," Maggie said. She smiled at Blake. "That was a wonderful thing to do."

Blake muttered, "No big deal," and looked embarrassed.

"Especially since everyone else was getting paid," Maggie said. "The woman said that she was sending checks for twenty-five dollars to the agents of all the elves."

Truly shook her head, looking puzzled. "No," she said. "My agent said we wouldn't get paid. He said the job was just for the experience I'd get."

"Maybe he didn't know about it. Maybe he'll get the check and be surprised." Maggie had forgotten what Truly had told her. She wished she hadn't brought it up.

"Maybe," Truly said slowly, as though she didn't believe it.

Roger leaned forward. "Margaret is probably right, Truly. Who is your agent?"

"Jerry Klinke," Truly answered.

Roger shook his head. "I don't know him," he said.

"He's supposed to be a good agent," Truly said anxiously. "His ad in the magazine listed all the things he did for his clients."

"His ad," Roger repeated, and frowned.

"Yes," Truly said. "And when he interviewed me, he said he had connections with casting directors, so it would be just a short time before I had parts in films or television. My father thought it over and said that the fee Mr. Klinke charged to handle me was worth it."

"Fee? He charged you a fee?"

"Five hundred dollars," Truly said. "It was supposed to be a thousand, but my father didn't have that much money, so Mr. Klinke said it was all right. He'd do us a favor and set things up so I could take acting jobs right away."

Roger mumbled something under his breath and scowled.

"Is something the matter?" Truly sounded whispery, as though she were frightened.

Roger suddenly patted Truly's shoulder and said, "As I told you, I don't know the man. I might just talk to your mother about him, though, when she comes to pick you up tonight."

"My father will probably come," Truly said.

"Fine. I'd like to meet him," Roger told her. He stood up and stretched. "I'll lend Kiki a hand. She might need someone to make the salad."

As he left the room, Truly turned to Maggie. "I don't understand," she murmured. "Something's wrong, isn't it?"

Blake jumped up, grabbed one of Maggie's hands and one of Truly's, and jerked them to their feet. "Let the adults take care of things like that," he said to Truly. "Do you realize you've been here almost all afternoon and you haven't gone out to look at the ocean?"

"Come on," Maggie said. "We can sit on the deck and watch the ocean gobble the sun."

"Where did you learn your true scientific facts?" Blake scoffed.

"Well, that's what it looks like," Maggie said. "The sun sits there for a whole minute, then—slurp!"

"When I was a really little girl," Truly said, "I thought the sun went down in a hole on the other side of a hill near our house." She giggled. "What did you think about the sunset when you were a little kid, Blake?"

Blake shrugged. "I guess I didn't think about it at all."

"Hurry up or we'll miss it!" Maggie yelled, and the three of them ran outside and leaned on the deck rail until the sky turned deep blue and the ocean was a glitter of softly swirling black spangles.

It was later, after the hot dogs and after Kiki had led them through every chorus of "The Twelve Days of Christmas" that Truly's father came to get her.

Maggie had forgotten the conversation about Truly's agent until some of her father's words to Mr. Norris were loud enough to carry out to the deck.

"Unscrupulous . . . no legitimate agent . . . shouldn't have charged a fee."

Truly looked so frightened that Maggie reached over and clasped her hand, holding it tightly.

Mr. Norris's voice was loud and angry. "I'll take care of him!"

"Oh, no!" Truly whispered to Maggie. "Sometimes my father has a terrible temper! Oh, Maggie, what's he going to do?"

Maggie's father might have wondered about that, too, because he attempted to calm Mr. Norris down before he left with Truly. A hot cup of coffee out on the deck, with the rhythm of the waves as a backup to the music Kiki strummed softly on her guitar, seemed to be just what Mr. Norris needed. He quietly thanked Roger and Kiki and reminded Truly to thank them, too.

Maggie grinned conspiratorily at Truly. When did parents wake up to the fact that their children could actually do things without being reminded?

"Come back soon," Kiki said as Truly scribbled her address and telephone number on a piece of paper and handed it to Maggie.

"I'll call you," Maggie said.

"Maybe you could come to our apartment. No, it's not very big, and—" Truly became so flustered that Maggie stepped in to help her out.

"Why don't we get together for a movie?" she asked.

"Good idea!" Truly looked as thankful as though she'd just

been pulled out of a leaky boat. Shyly she said good-bye to Blake, as though she'd suddenly remembered that he was a celebrity. Blake, who had disappeared behind his Dick Dackery smile, wasn't any help.

"Thanks again," Mr. Norris said, and they left.

Maggie immediately turned to her father. "Tell me," she said. "What's the matter with Truly's agent?"

"Obviously he's not a legitimate agent," Roger told her. "An agent doesn't charge money up front. He takes only a percentage of any fees earned by an actor, usually ten to twenty percent."

"But, according to Truly, in Mr. Klinke's ad he listed all the jobs he's found for his clients."

"That's another thing," Roger said. "A good agent doesn't advertise." He shook his head. "I'm afraid that Klinke is just another unscrupulous person taking advantage of people who are desperate to become successful actors and don't know how the system works."

"Then shouldn't he be arrested?"

"I'm afraid that when Norris reads the contract he signed with Klinke, he'll discover that Klinke legally covered himself."

"But what about the twenty-five dollars the hospital guild is going to send him for Truly? He'll be stealing it."

"I can't guess about that. He's probably covered himself there, too."

"It's not fair!" Maggie said. "He took their money, and he lied to them and cheated them! Why can't they have him arrested?"

"Because he's done what he's promised. He's sent Truly out on a few jobs and a few auditions, hasn't he?"

"Yes."

"I'm sorry, Margaret," Roger said. "I'm afraid there isn't much more that can be done."

"Daddy!" Maggie said. "Why don't you give Truly a part in your next picture?"

"Because there are no parts for little girls in it," Roger said.

"Maybe you could write one in."

"Isn't it your bedtime?" Roger asked.

"I know it's mine," Blake said. "I've got to be on the set at 6 A.M."

"You have to work tomorrow? But it's Christmas vacation," Maggie said.

"For you," Blake said. "Not for me. I have some makeup shots, a few close-up scenes to do over for the last two shows of the season."

With Dick Dackery poise and charm, he shook hands with Roger, Kiki, and Maggie and left.

Maggie slumped at one end of the sofa. She didn't like Dick Dackery. She liked Blake. And she didn't like what was happening to her friend Truly. And, at the moment, she didn't even like the Christmas tree.

"Could I call Grandma and talk to her for a little while?" she blurted out.

Roger looked at his watch. "You'd wake her up. There's a two-hour time difference between the West Coast and Houston."

Maggie felt her eyes grow moist, and she gave a loud sniff, trying to hold back the tears.

"Where's the television guide?" Kiki asked. "We can watch something on TV."

"No, thanks," Maggie said. She climbed out of the low sofa. "I think I'll go to bed." She sighed. "Maybe I'll dream up some way to help Truly."

"She had a good time today, Maggie," Kiki said. "You gave her that."

"So did you." With a shock Maggie suddenly realized what else she should have said. Maybe parents were right in nudging their children. "Uh—Kiki, thank you for getting the tree and the ornaments and for making so much fun for everyone."

Kiki beamed. "I had just as much fun as the rest of you."

Maggie warmed to the subject. "You were like one of us. Well, you really are, I guess. You're sort of a big sister since you're just a few years older than we are."

Kiki's glance fluttered off to one side, and Roger's lips tightened as his face reddened. Maggie wanted to groan. *Why can't I keep my mouth shut?* she silently asked herself. *I didn't mean to make my father angry. I didn't want to embarrass Kiki.*

Quickly she stammered, "Good night, Daddy. Good night, Kiki," and fled toward her bedroom.

In the morning the telephone woke her. She heard mumbled voices as her father answered. Then came a tap on her door.

"Margaret," her father said, "it's for you."

Maggie fumbled for the telephone on her bedside table. "Grandma?" she shouted eagerly into the phone.

"No," a woebegone voice answered. "It's me—Truly."

"Oh," Maggie said, wishing it had been her grandmother.

"Maggie, something terrible happened." There was a pause as Truly gave a little sob.

"What happened?" Maggie clutched the receiver so tightly that her fingers hurt. She waited but heard only a muffled silence. "Truly?" she shouted. "Are you still there?"

"Yes," came a small voice, and Truly said, "Maggie, I'm trying not to cry."

"Okay," Maggie said. "I understand. You just scared me, that's all. Can't you tell me what's the matter?"

"It's hard," Truly said. She seemed to take a long, deep

breath, then her words spilled out quickly. "My father's in jail!"

Maggie jumped up, but her legs began to wobble as though the bones had suddenly turned to cooked spaghetti. She quickly dropped down on the bed, still holding tightly to the receiver. "Why?" she asked.

"He went to Mr. Klinke's office to talk to him, and he lost his temper—my father, that is—and he hit Mr. Klinke and gave him a black eye. Then Mr. Klinke called the police and had my father arrested."

"Mr. Klinke's the one who should have been arrested!" Maggie exploded.

"I wish Dad hadn't lost his temper."

"It doesn't do any good to wish. What we need to do is think about how we can help your father."

"That's what *your* father would have said," Truly told her. "I guess you and your father think alike. You really are a lot alike."

"No, we're not! We don't even look alike."

"I didn't mean to make you mad, and I didn't mean that you look alike. You don't look anything alike. It's your personalities. That's where I think you're very much like your father."

Maggie swallowed her indignation and made herself calm down. "Forget about that, Truly," she said. "What's important is your father. He can't stay in jail."

"Mom is taking care of getting him out," Truly explained. "She borrowed money to pay Dad's bail, and she went down to the police station to drive him home."

"What happens next?"

"Mom said that Dad will have to appear in court, and Mr. Klinke will come and accuse him of hitting him, and the judge might send Dad to jail, or fine him, or both."

"What would happen if Mr. Klinke didn't accuse him?"

"I don't know," Truly said. "Do you think that Dad would go free then?"

Maggie suddenly decided what to do. "What time is it?" she asked.

"Almost ten o'clock," Truly said. "Why?"

"It's twelve o'clock then in Houston," Maggie said. "I've got to talk to somebody, Truly. I'll call you back in a little while. Maybe we can come up with something to help your father."

Immediately she dialed Grandma's number and was so excited when she heard her grandmother's familiar voice that she practically shouted, "Grandma!"

"Maggie!" Grandma shouted back. "Little love, how are you?"

In the background Maggie could hear voices chattering and an occasional shout and squeal. "Is everybody there at your house?" Maggie asked, feeling so left out that her stomach began to ache.

"Just about," Grandma said, "although I think we're missing the mailman and two neighbors who live down on the corner." She raised her voice over those in the room and said to them, "Be quiet for a few minutes! Maggie's on the phone, and I can't hear her!"

The babble became louder. "They all send you their love," Grandma yelled. "No, you can't talk to Maggie right now, Jason. Somebody put Flowerpot outside. She's eating my sandwich. Debbie, move that glass of milk before you— Oh, dear. Will someone please get a towel and mop up that milk?"

"Grandma, I need to talk to you," Maggie said.

"Hang on, Maggie," Grandma said. "I'm going to get this in my bedroom, where there's some peace and quiet. I'll put Debbie on until I get there."

Debbie screeched into Maggie's ear, "Hi, Maggie! Jason got

into the chocolate fudge last night when Mama didn't know about it, and he ate too much and threw up!"

"Hi, Debbie." Maggie couldn't help giggling. "I miss you."

"I miss you, too," Debbie said. "Would you like me to tell you the poem I learned in school?"

"Not right now, dear," Grandma said firmly on the extension. "You may hang up."

"Good-bye, Maggie," Debbie yelled. There was a loud click and a peaceful silence.

"There we are," Grandma said to Maggie. "It's so good to talk to you. Are you having fun?"

"Yes," Maggie said, surprising herself. "Yes. I guess I am. We decorated a Christmas tree yesterday. It's kind of like yours, and I met a couple of kids my age, and they're nice, and that's what I wanted to talk to you about."

She told Grandma about Truly and her agent, trying to remember everything that Roger had said, then told her about Mr. Norris and what he had done.

"Obviously," Grandma said, "Mr. Klinke is a criminal himself and ought to be locked up. But Roger is right. He's probably protected himself legally. However—"

This is what Maggie had been waiting for. She leaned forward eagerly. "However what, Grandma?"

"However," Grandma said, "from the mystery novels I've read, I've learned something important, which is that criminals usually make mistakes. Mr. Klinke may be stealing money from people who come to California to get into the movies and don't know how to go about it, but somewhere along the line he's bound to be making a mistake. The trick is to figure out what kind of mistake he's making."

"How?" Maggie asked.

"I don't know," Grandma said, and sighed. "It makes me furious to think about how many innocent people must come to Mr. Klinke's office with hopes and dreams, and over and over he robs them of their money and their dreams. Somewhere along the line he must make a mistake in what he says or does. I just wish there was some way to find out."

"Grandma!" Maggie said. "You gave me a great idea!"

"I did?"

"Yes," Maggie said. "I can't tell you what it is yet because I have to think some more about it, but I'll call you and tell you if it works."

"Don't do anything rash," Grandma cautioned. "Be sure to discuss this with—"

Maggie interrupted. "I promise, Grandma, that I won't do anything without talking it over with Dad or Kiki."

"Good," Grandma said. She sounded relieved. "I'll look forward to hearing from you, honey. I love you."

"I love you, too, Grandma," Maggie said.

As Maggie hung up the receiver, she smiled. Kiki was going to be a part of this idea. All Maggie had to do was to talk her into it.

8

"Don't you see?" she told Kiki later. "It's the only way we can find out."

The breeze from the ocean was sticky with salt against Maggie's skin; and the sun, which had battled the early morning fog and won, was warming her back. She put down her half-eaten piece of buttered toast and discovered that her paper napkin had blown off her lap, so she wiped her hands on her shorts and said, "Think about it. It's our best chance for finding out."

Kiki, her tanned legs propped against the deck railing, brushed a strand of her long blond hair back from her face and said, "I am thinking."

Maggie fidgeted until Kiki swung her legs down and turned to pick up her coffee cup. "My first thought was that we should discuss this idea of yours with Roger. But I honestly can't see any problems with it."

"And Daddy isn't going to be home until late tonight." Maggie leaned toward Kiki. "Will you do it?"

"There's an alternative," Kiki said. "We could ask Truly to

tell us in detail everything about her first interview with Mr. Klinke."

"But she might forget something important because she wouldn't know it was important."

Kiki nodded. "That's true." She leaned back in her chair and said, "Okay. Let's go for it. But first, we'll have to plan this step by step."

"Right!" Maggie bounced in her chair. "You'll be the mother, and I'll be your daughter. Only you'll have to"—she hesitated and added in a small voice—"make yourself look older."

Kiki smiled as though what Maggie had blurted out the night before had never happened. "I can do that with makeup. No problem." She giggled. "I'd better wear a wig."

"You can call Mr. Klinke's office in a few minutes and make an appointment. Make it as soon as he can see us. And when we get there, you can tell him that we came to Los Angeles so I could become a film actress."

"Where are we from? We'll have to get everything straight."

"Houston? No. He'd expect us to have some kind of western accent."

"How about from a town in Arizona? Like Kingman?"

"That sounds good." Maggie paused. "Why did you pick Kingman?"

"Because that's my own hometown," Kiki said.

"I don't know much about you," Maggie admitted.

"Nor I about you," Kiki said. "But we'll have time while you're here to find out. That is, if you'd like to."

"Yes," Maggie said. "I would."

"Okay, back to business," Kiki said. "What about your credits? We won't have a scrapbook of your press clippings or anything like that."

"I don't think we'll need one," Maggie said. "I doubt if Mr. Klinke is very particular about whom he cheats."

Kiki nodded. "Have we covered it? Can you think of anything else?"

"I think we should take a tape recorder and record every word. We might even need it as some kind of proof."

"That's a great idea. I've got a little one I can carry in my handbag."

"Speaking of handbags," Maggie said. "You can't—that is, your clothes are—ummm." She didn't know how to phrase what she wanted to say.

But Kiki understood. "Don't worry. I won't walk into Klinke's office swinging a bag with a designer label." She stood up. "I'll make the call now. No point in waiting any longer."

Maggie stood next to her as she got Klinke's telephone number and address from the operator and made the call. But an answering service took the call.

"His office will be open in five minutes," Kiki said. "I didn't leave a number with the service. I'll just call again."

It was hard for Maggie to wait, but finally the five minutes were up, and apparently Mr. Klinke's secretary answered because Kiki said, "I'd like to make an appointment for a meeting with Mr. Klinke. My daughter's very talented, and I think she has a real future in movies and television."

She was silent for a moment; then her eyes opened wide, and she stammered, "Uh—Barbara Jones. My daughter is named Leslie."

There was another pause, then Kiki said, "Eleven-thirty?" She looked at her watch. "Yes. We can be there by then."

She waited again, and Maggie wished she could hear the whole conversation, especially when Kiki said, "Oh, I can't give you a phone number. The hotel we're staying in doesn't have phones in the rooms, so I'm calling from a pay phone. But don't worry. We'll keep our appointment on time. I'm eager to talk to Mr. Klinke."

Once more Kiki listened, then said, "Oh, we found out about Mr. Klinke through his ad in the magazine." Rapidly she added, "I've got to go now. Someone's waiting to use this phone. Good-bye."

She put down the receiver and said, "I was afraid she was going to ask what magazine. Did Truly tell you?"

"No," Maggie said. "I'll call her and ask. Is it all right if I tell her what we're going to do?"

"Better not," Kiki said. "For now I think we should keep it between ourselves."

Jerry Klinke's office was on the second floor of a small office building on Hollywood Boulevard, near Highland Avenue. The stairway was narrow, and the wooden railing was worn and smudged where the reddish brown stain had been rubbed away.

It wasn't hard to find his office. It was near the top of the stairs, and his name was stenciled in gold paint on the opaque glass. Maggie took a deep breath and followed Kiki as she opened the door and led the way into the office.

Both Kiki and Maggie were dressed in simple blouses and skirts. Kiki also wore an old yellow cardigan sweater with a small hole in one elbow. Maggie thought Kiki was overdoing it a bit, but after Kiki had aged her face with theatrical makeup and put on a dark wig with a nondescript hairstyle, she had enthusiastically plunged into the part.

The plump middle-aged woman who sat behind the desk was even less fashionable than Kiki. She smiled at them vacantly as Kiki repeated their names: Barbara and Leslie Jones.

"Just take a seat." The woman waved toward a row of chrome-and-green plastic chairs, which were lined against one wall.

As they sat down behind a round wooden coffee table piled with old issues of *Hollywood Reporter* and *Variety*, Maggie

studied the small room. Two large plastic plants were sta-
tioned on either side of the door like limp, dusty sentries,
and rows of framed photographs decorated the wall behind
the secretary's desk. Maggie walked over to examine them.
The smiling faces belonged to people of all ages, and most
of the photographs were signed. Maybe these were some of
Mr. Klinke's clients. Maggie didn't recognize any of them.

The secretary pointed to one of the photographs. "Third
from the left," she said. "You probably saw him in that big
dog-food commercial."

Maggie studied the boy's face and shook her head.

"Well," the secretary said, "you ought to watch more TV."

A buzzer sounded on her desk, and she picked up the telephone. "Yes, they're here, Mr. Klinke," she said. She put down
the phone and motioned toward the door on the far side of
the room. "You can see Mr. Klinke now. Good luck."

"Thanks," Maggie said. She saw Kiki open the clasp of the
small straw handbag she was carrying and knew she was
turning on the tape recorder. Maggie rubbed her damp palms
down the sides of her skirt and hoped Mr. Klinke wouldn't
notice how nervous she was as she opened the door and entered his office.

Jerry Klinke was short and balding. His eyes were shielded
with huge, very dark sunglasses, but a little of the discolor-
ation around his left eye managed to show. He wore a striped
three-piece suit, and the buttons that strained to hold his vest
looked as though they'd pop off at any minute. He didn't stand
as they came in. He just swiveled sideways in his chair, seemed
to take a long hard look at them, and brushed aside a few
papers on his messy desk.

Without waiting to be invited, Kiki sat in one of the chairs
facing his desk, and Maggie sat in the other.

Klinke leaned forward, and it was obvious that he was staring at Kiki. Finally he said, "You look kind of young to be this kid's mother."

Kiki simply beamed and said, "Oh, thank you!"

Apparently Klinke was satisfied because he seemed to relax, leaning back in his chair, and said to Kiki, "So you want your kid to get into movies."

"Yes," Kiki said.

"So do lots and lots of people," Klinke said. "We get 'em in here every day, day after day, everybody hoping their kids will end up rich and famous. You probably got the same idea."

"Leslie is very talented," Kiki said.

"Yeah? What's she done?"

"She's been in school plays, and she sings and dances a little."

"Just a little?"

"We plan to have her take lessons, now that we're here in Hollywood," Kiki said quickly.

"Good idea," Klinke said. "I'll sign her up with an acting school. They're a little high, but it's worth it. I send a lot of people there, so they give my clients a discount. To make it easier for you, you can pay me." He mentioned a price.

"What's the name of the school?" Kiki asked. Klinke looked a little surprised, but he told her. Then Kiki said, "I heard about another school. Someone told me it has a fine reputation." She named the most famous acting school in Southern California.

Klinke shook his head. "No good. Your kid won't get anywhere there. If you want me to handle her, you'll have to cooperate, Mrs. Jones. I like my clients to study at the same place."

"All right," Kiki said. "I was just asking."

The telephone rang, and Klinke picked up the receiver. "Yeah," he said. "How about the Polo Lounge, four o'clock?

Sure. They know me there. That's where I make some of my best deals."

Klinke hung up and turned to Maggie. "Leslie," he said, "tell me something about your stage experience. So far I don't even know if you can talk."

"I can talk," Maggie said. "And I can sing. I played the part of Brigitta in *The Sound of Music*, and I was one of the orphans in *Annie*. Would you like to hear me sing?"

"I'll take your word for it." He leaned his elbows on the desk and scowled. "Acting is hard work and long hours, kid. It's not all glamour. You understand that?"

Maggie nodded.

"And as I said, there are hundreds of people out there for every job."

"Maybe we'd better just give up and go back to Arizona," Kiki said with a long, discouraged sigh that made Maggie want to giggle.

Klinke quickly said, "No! You're in the right hands here. The whole secret of success is in teaming up with an agent who can do things for you. And your kid looks good. There are lots of parts right now for young teenagers. I don't see any reason why she won't make it to the top."

"Wow!" Maggie said. "Really?"

"It's almost impossible for an unknown to get accepted by an agent, but this is your lucky day. I'm willing to take a chance because I believe that Leslie could be a star."

"Me? A star?" Maggie tried not to choke on the words.

"So Lois, my secretary, will have some papers for you to sign, and we'll need glossy photos which I can—"

Kiki interrupted. "But you haven't told us just what you will do for Leslie. We don't know what to expect."

"Do?" Klinke asked. He shrugged. "Well, for one thing, as I said, we'll get her into acting school and get a portfolio made.

Did I tell you I can get you a discount with a top photographer?
To make it even easier for you, you can just pay me."

"All right," Kiki said. "What photographer is it?"

"He's a friend of mine," Klinke said. "His name doesn't
matter, does it?"

Maggie held her breath. Klinke was beginning to stare sus-
piciously at Kiki. But Kiki just looked pleasant and said, "I'm
sorry. I'm asking too many questions. This is just such a big
move for us, and I'm so eager for Leslie to succeed as an
actress."

Maggie jumped in. "Will I go on auditions at movie
studios?"

"Sure you will," Klinke said. "I'm in touch with all the
casting directors, so I'll send you out to try for any part that
suits your age."

"Will I make lots of money?"

"Sure, if you work hard."

"Oh, I will!" Maggie said.

"And speaking of money," Klinke said, "my fee for handling
you is fifteen hundred dollars."

Maggie and Kiki both gasped. Kiki recovered first. "We
don't have that much money."

Klinke rested his chin on his hands and scowled down at
his desk for a few minutes. Finally he raised his head, stared
through his big dark glasses at Kiki, and said, "Just what are
you doing in my office?"

9

Kiki tensed as though she were ready to jump up and run. "What do you mean?" she asked.

"I mean that you don't expect me to work to promote this kid for nothing, do you?"

"Oh, no!" Kiki said. "It's just that I didn't anticipate that your—uh—fee would be that much."

He swiveled his chair around so that his back was to them, and he stared at the windowless wall behind his desk. Maggie looked at Kiki, but Kiki just shrugged. They waited.

He turned back to face them, and his tone was genial. "Okay," he said. "I've thought it over. As I said, I like your kid. I believe in her future. Suppose, as a special favor to you, I cut my fee?"

"Oh, thank you," Kiki said.

"How about seven-fifty? Can you make that?"

"I—I think so," Kiki answered. Maggie heard her gulp. "And for that seven hundred and fifty dollars you'll—"

The telephone rang, interrupting her. Klinke held up a hand to stop her and answered the phone.

"Klinke here," he said. "Yeah. I called you earlier about that department store promotion. I heard you'd be needing three more kids for it. Does it matter where I heard it? I can have them there. Girls, junior sizes, right? What are we talking about? Under scale, of course. Fifty apiece? Okay. I'll put my secretary on. She'll work out the details."

He hung up and turned back to Kiki. "Sorry," he said. "Where were we? I've got so many deals going right now that if I get interrupted, I lose my train of thought."

Kiki said, "I think you were saying that we had to fill out some papers."

"Oh, yeah. Right. It's just a simple contract. Lots of legal gobbledegook that spells out what we are talking about. You don't even have to waste time reading it." He pressed a button and, when Lois answered, said, "Pull a contract out for Leslie Jones and her mother. Yeah. Get both signatures." He leaned back and pointed to the door. "Glad to meet you. Glad to do business with you. Lois will tell you everything you'll need to do."

Kiki stood, and Maggie followed her lead. "Will Leslie get a job soon?" Kiki asked.

"Yeah. Soon as something comes up."

"How about that one with the department store promotion we heard you talking about a few minutes ago?"

His eyebrows dipped into a scowl, almost disappearing behind his sunglasses. "Wrong age," he said quickly. "Yeah. They want little kids."

"The fifty dollars would have been a big help." Kiki sighed pitifully, and Maggie hoped she wasn't overdoing the act. "They were paying fifty dollars, weren't they?"

"You ask an awful lot of questions." Klinke scowled. *He's suspicious of us,* Maggie thought.

But Klinke suddenly said, "I've got some calls to make. Just go out there and sign the stuff Lois gives you. You can pay her with cash or a check."

Now what? Maggie wondered. How would Kiki handle this? Surely she wouldn't give them any money.

The contracts were on Lois's desk. With a bored yawn she shoved them at Kiki. "Sign on the last page of both copies," she said.

Kiki picked them up. "I'll read them first."

Lois looked surprised. "Okay. I never met anybody yet who could understand all that legal stuff. I doubt if you can."

"Could I take these with me? I'd like to have my husband read them before I sign them."

"No!" Lois was adamant. "Mr. Klinke won't let them out of his office until after they're signed."

Kiki gave Maggie a quick glance. She was telling Maggie something. Maggie just hoped she had got the right message. She leaned on Lois's desk. "Tell me about the people in the photographs," she said. "Are they all famous?" She pointed to a picture of a girl her age. "What's her name? What does she do? Is she in movies or television?"

Lois turned around to look. "Her? Uh—I forget her name. Can you read her signature?"

Maggie stood under the picture and squinted. "I can't tell. Is this an 'R' or a 'B'?"

Lois stood with her nose close to the photograph. "It's a 'B.' I don't know why you couldn't read it."

Kiki's voice interrupted them. "Here's your contract. I put it on the end of the desk."

"Okay," Lois said, taking her seat again. "I'll need payment for Mr. Klinke's fee, for the lessons and the photographs of Leslie. You want to pay cash or write a check?"

"Nothing right now," Kiki said, "and I didn't sign the contracts. I want to talk this over with my husband."

"You didn't give me your phone number or address," Lois

said. "Mr. Klinke will want me to have those in any case."

"Ummm, not today," Kiki said. She grabbed Maggie's hand and edged toward the door.

"What is this?" Lois asked. She picked up the contract and realized there was only one in her hand. "What are you up to?"

Kiki quickly opened the door. "Thanks for all your help," she called. "I'll be in touch."

They clattered down the stairs and were out on the street before Kiki stopped to tell Maggie, "While you were distracting Lois, I tucked one of the contracts into my handbag."

"What should we do next?" Maggie asked. "Talk to Dad about it?"

Kiki smiled. "Better yet. I know a detective on the Beverly Hills police force. Bill Hartley. He worked as consultant on a film I was in. Let's go home so I can take off this makeup. We'll make sandwiches for lunch. Then I'll call Bill. If he has some free time, we can go to his office, tell him all about Klinke, and play the tape for him. Maybe we can get this guy arrested."

But after they had finished their story and played the tape, Detective Hartley just shook his head. "This tape would not hold up in court. Don't you know it's illegal to secretly tape a conversation to use against an individual?"

"I didn't know," Kiki said.

"Could we be arrested?" Maggie asked.

"You'd be arrested if you made the tape public and Mr. Klinke brought charges against you."

"We won't," Maggie said quickly. Darn! She thought about the tape. There was something on it that bothered her, but she didn't know what it was. It was something that Mr. Klinke had said. What was it?

Detective Hartley thumbed through the contract, skimming

it. Finally he dropped the contract on his desk and leaned back in his chair, hands clasped behind his head. "That's it?" he asked.

"Isn't it enough?" Maggie leaned forward eagerly.

"I'm afraid not," he said.

"But Bill," Kiki said, "you heard Klinke. He is charging people for acting lessons and photographs and topping it all off with a big fee!"

"That's not illegal, as it stands," he said.

"What does that mean?"

"Well, if he's telling people he can get them a discount with the acting school, then overcharging them, he could possibly get in trouble there. But you might run into a problem. If whoever operates the school is working a scam with Klinke, he'll back up Klinke's story."

"Mr. Klinke's a crook!" Maggie said. "He didn't pay Truly the twenty-five dollars he was supposed to pay her when she worked as an elf for that hospital program."

"Did he have an answer for that?" Detective Hartley asked.

"Yes," Maggie said reluctantly. "Truly told me this morning that Mr. Klinke told her father that he used the twenty-five dollars to pay himself back for all the extra expenses, phone calls, and other things he did to further Truly's career."

"You might get him on that point," Detective Hartley said. "If Truly's parents could hire an attorney and file a suit against Klinke, their attorney could ask that Klinke's books be subpoenaed. He'd have to prove the charges."

"I don't think they could afford to do that," Maggie said.

Detective Hartley sat upright. "They probably wouldn't want to, either," he said. "A civil suit can be a long, drawn-out process, and it's a gamble. They could lose it and be out a great deal of money."

"Darn," Kiki said. "So you can't do a single thing to stop that man."

"I couldn't anyway," Detective Hartley said. "You said his office is in Hollywood, and that would be under the jurisdiction of the Los Angeles police. My territory is Beverly Hills."

"It's so unfair that he can get away with what he's doing!" Kiki said. She picked up the contract, tucked it into her handbag, and stood up.

Something tickled the back of Maggie's mind. She wished they could play that tape again. There was something in it that she was sure they missed.

"I'm sorry we took up so much of your time," Kiki told him. "You were very kind to listen to all this and advise us."

"Yes," Maggie agreed as she walked to the door of Detective Hartley's office. "Thank you."

"Glad to do it," Detective Hartley said. "If you have any more questions or come up with anything else, just give me a call, although I think you're fighting a lost cause with this one."

"We'll see," Kiki answered and smiled.

"There's one thing I can do for you," Detective Hartley said. "I'll run a computer check on the guy. We'll find out about his past, if he's got a record of any arrests or convictions. We might turn up something that will help."

Maggie didn't know how Kiki could look so calm and cheerful. Maggie had never felt so discouraged. She trailed after Kiki to the parking lot and climbed into the passenger side of Kiki's car.

"I know there's something on that tape that will help us," Maggie said. "But I don't know what it is."

"Let's go to Rodeo Drive," Kiki said. "We need to get our minds off this situation for a little while. Then we can get back to it with a fresh approach."

"What's on Rodeo Drive besides shops?" Maggie asked.

Kiki stopped at the booth, handed the attendant her ticket and money, then blinked at Maggie. "Besides shops! Don't you love to browse through shops and look at clothes?"

Maggie shrugged. "It's okay if I've got to buy something."

"But all the beautiful Christmas merchandise is on display, and the decorations are lovely." Kiki accepted her change from the attendant, dropped it into her open handbag, and drove onto the street. She gave Maggie a quick glance and added, "Also, I know a place in the Rodeo Collection where we can get some super-good ice cream."

"Sometimes ice cream helps me think," Maggie said, and the two of them burst into laughter.

"Shopping first," Kiki said, "because it was *my* idea."

Maggie leaned back against the seat and absentmindedly counted the large painted snowflakes of metal and lights that decorated the lampposts along Wilshire Boulevard. Soon Kiki turned down Rodeo Drive. Along the median stretched a brilliant band of red poinsettias, from which rose cone-shaped trees sprouting huge bows of red ribbon.

"I can't believe it," Kiki said. "A parking place!" and she neatly maneuvered into a spot in front of a shop called Polo and fished some change for the meter out of her bag.

Maggie followed Kiki into Polo and a couple of nearby shops, and into one across the street called Jax, which sold T-shirts with *Rodeo Drive* printed on the front. Maggie began to perk up. "I could buy one as a souvenir for Lisa," she told Kiki. "And one for Grandma."

Kiki's eyes widened. "Shouldn't you get Mrs. Landry something a little more—uh—grandmotherly?"

"You don't know Grandma very well," Maggie said. "She'd like the T-shirt. She could wear it when she goes jogging." Maggie left the shop with two of the shirts, a blue one for

Lisa to match her eyes and a kelly green one for Grandma.

Kiki dropped another handful of change into the parking meter and walked briskly in the direction of Santa Monica. It took just a few minutes to get to the Rodeo Collection, which was a three-story cluster of shops around a beautiful, plant-filled, open atrium. They went directly to the place Kiki had mentioned, ordered double-scoop dishes, and sat at an empty table outside on the balcony.

Maggie took a small bite, closing her eyes as the deep chocolate flavor shivered on her tongue. Kiki had been right. She was relaxed now and ready to think again about what Mr. Klinke had said.

"Could we play the tape now?" she asked, and Kiki took the little recorder out of her handbag, placing it between them, turning it on and keeping the volume low.

Maggie, who was listening very carefully to every word, began to get discouraged as nothing happened to jog her thoughts. They were almost at the end of the conversation in Mr. Klinke's office, and Maggie had picked up her spoon to take another bite of ice cream when something in her mind said, *This is it!*

She dropped her spoon and jumped to her feet. "Kiki!" she said. "I think we've found the answer!"

10

"What answer?" Kiki looked confused.

"We were concentrating on what Mr. Klinke was telling *us*," Maggie explained. "So we weren't paying that much attention to everything he said during his telephone call. Now listen again." She sat down again, ran the tape back just a bit, then pressed the play button.

They heard Kiki talking about the seven hundred fifty dollars, until she was interrupted by the ring of the telephone and the now familiar voice.

"Klinke here. Yeah. I called you earlier about that department store promotion. I heard you'd be needing three more kids for it. Does it matter where I heard it? I can have them there. Girls, junior sizes, right? What are we talking about? Under scale, of course. Fifty apiece? Okay. I'll put my secretary on. She'll work out the details."

Maggie pressed the stop button, and Kiki said, "I don't get it."

"You will," Maggie said. "Wait until you hear the rest." Using fast forward, she moved the tape ahead, missing the place she wanted the first time, then trying again. Finally she nodded with satisfaction and let the tape play. Klinke's voice came in clearly: "Wrong age. Yeah. They want little kids." Once more she stopped the tape.

Kiki frowned. "Wait a minute. Klinke said first something about girls wearing junior sizes. Then he said 'little kids.' That doesn't make sense."

"Now it does," Maggie told her. "He said that about the little kids because he didn't want to send me on the job. I knew about that payment of fifty dollars per person. I'll bet that Mr. Klinke's clients won't see any of that money."

"I wish we could find out. It's too bad that Truly's no longer one of his clients. He might have sent her on that job."

"We need to talk to Truly," Maggie said. "She might be able to tell us the names of some of Klinke's other clients."

Kiki nodded enthusiastically. "She could tell us other non-paying jobs he sent her on. And the others could. And we could check to see what they were paid."

A couple sat down at the table next to them, and Maggie lowered her voice. "Let's go, Kiki! Let's get busy!"

"You haven't eaten all your ice cream," Kiki said.

Maggie looked at the dark, satiny ice cream. She couldn't believe she had forgotten all about it. "Well, we could wait a couple of minutes," she said, and dug her spoon into the frozen mound.

Truly was at her apartment in West Hollywood when Maggie telephoned, but her parents were out. Her mother had gone back to work, and her father was out running errands. She invited them to come right away.

The rooms of the Norris apartment were small but sunny and overlooked a tiny garden, where a large elm tree spread out its branches like fat fingers, protecting ragged patches of multicolored pansies. The sofas and chairs in the apartment were decorated with puffy, bright pillows, and some framed black-and-white glossy studio shots of Truly rested on top of the television set. A small artificial Christmas tree stood in the corner. There were only a few ornaments on it, but some brightly wrapped packages were piled underneath.

Kiki stood by the open window. "I love your garden," she said.

"I do, too," Truly said. "Dad planted the pansies, and I try to remember to water them."

Maggie sat down without being invited. "Kiki and I have a lot to tell you," she said.

"Go ahead." As soon as Kiki had found a chair, Truly perched on the sofa next to Maggie. She hugged a pillow and listened to what they had to say. Then she listened to the tape. "Mr. Klinke told you almost the same thing that he told us," she said.

"Did you pay him for acting lessons and photographs?" Kiki asked.

Truly nodded. "I guess we wasted the money. I wish we'd known how legitimate agents work."

Kiki reached over and patted her hand. "Maybe we can get some of that money back for you. We're going to try."

Maggie asked, "Truly, can you give us a list of the other just-for-experience jobs Klinke has sent you on? And the names of some of his other clients who've had the same dealings with him that you've had?"

Truly nodded. "There's Cary. He was one of the elves. And a girl named Billie—Billie Martin, who ran down the hill with a bunch of kids when we were doing that gum commercial. And Jan. She was in that commercial, too."

Kiki took a pencil and pad and wrote down the names of the companies involved and the dates of the events. She tore off the paper and waved it as though it were a flag. "We're making progress!" she said.

"I can give you Billie's address," Truly said. "She lives near here."

"Good," Kiki said. "It's a start."

Truly sighed. "I don't understand what you're doing. I don't know how it will help my father."

"If we can get enough proof that Klinke is defrauding his clients and they take action against him, it can put a stop to what he's doing," Kiki said. "And with a lawsuit facing him, he might be willing to drop the charges against your father."

Maggie glanced at the Christmas tree. "It's just two days until Christmas," she said, "and Klinke is like Scrooge. I wish he could be visited by the three ghosts, who would show him the error of his ways, the way Scrooge was."

"Will you settle for three very live ghosts—you, Truly, and me?" Kiki asked.

Truly hopped up. "With some gray-and-white face makeup, we could—"

"No," Kiki said. "It might be fun, but we're dealing with a modern Scrooge, and we're going to go about this in a logical, modern way."

A key rattled the front-door lock, and the door swung open. Mr. Norris stepped into the room. He was carrying two large bags of groceries. Startled by the visitors, he nearly dropped one of the bags but managed to put them on the nearest table.

"Mrs.—Mrs. Ledoux!" he stammered. "Maggie! It's nice of you to pay us a visit. Truly, didn't you offer our guests something to eat? Some cookies? A soft drink?"

Kiki stood and with her easy smile took Mr. Norris's hand, leading him to a chair as though she were the hostess. She went over the situation with Klinke and told Mr. Norris what she and Maggie wanted to do.

Maggie expected Mr. Norris to be overjoyed, but instead he frowned and rubbed his chin. Finally he said, "From what that detective told you, there doesn't seem to be any way we could get our money back short of going to court and suing him. I can't see getting involved in a legal suit."

"But he cheated you!" Maggie said.

"If you and some of the parents of his other clients were to get together on legal action—" Kiki began.

But Mr. Norris interrupted her. He leaned forward, resting his forearms on his legs and clasping his hands so tightly that his knuckles turned white. "Mrs. Ledoux," he said, "I appreciate your help. I sincerely do. But I had some time to think about all this while I was sitting in that jail. I was wrong to lose my temper. All it did was cause a lot of trouble, and when my case comes up, who knows—I'll probably have to pay a big fine and might even end up in jail once more. If I have any more dealings with that man, I may lose my temper again."

"But if an attorney—"

"It's going to cost me enough just to defend myself in court."

Maggie spoke up. "Mr. Norris, we want to stop Mr. Klinke from cheating people. And we want him to drop charges against you. Don't you want that, too?"

Mr. Norris just stared down at his hands. Maggie held her breath and waited.

11

Finally Mr. Norris raised his head. "There's something else I'd better tell you. Betty and I—Betty's my wife—had a long talk about this whole Hollywood business, and we decided that after this mess I'm in is taken care of, we're going to move back home to Montana."

Truly gasped and jumped to her feet. "But, Dad! What about my acting career?"

Maggie didn't know which one looked more miserable, Mr. Norris or Truly, as he said, "Honey, we can't keep this up. I made a bad move in signing you with Klinke and lost a lot of money in the process."

"But I can earn it back when I get acting jobs!"

"That might take a while," Mr. Norris said, "and there are no guarantees."

"But, Dad—"

"I didn't mean to spring it on you like this, honey," he said. "When your mother comes home, she can explain it better than I can."

Kiki said firmly, "Mr. Norris, we're trying to help you."

He turned to Kiki. "I appreciate what you're doing."

"Then let's work together. I'm sure that you're not the only one whom Klinke has cheated."

Mr. Norris thought a moment, then said, "I'll do whatever I can—to a point."

"Don't give up," Kiki said. "I'll call you tomorrow, after I've talked to the parents of some of the other children who I think are being cheated by Klinke, too."

Maggie was so uncomfortable and embarrassed that she was glad to leave the Norris apartment. "Let's go home," she said.

Kiki looked at the piece of notepaper in her hand. "Why don't we call on Billie Martin and her mother first? They live just a few blocks from here."

"Maybe they'll be as unhappy as Mr. Norris. Maybe they won't want to talk to us. Maybe they won't be home," Maggie said.

"Any other excuses for not going?" Kiki said.

Maggie sighed. "I guess I'm trying to get out of seeing them because I don't know what to expect."

"What do you want to do?"

"Help Truly." Maggie opened the door of Kiki's car. "Ready? We can see if Mrs. Martin and Billie want to talk to us."

Mrs. Martin was more than willing to invite Maggie and Kiki in. It was obvious that she knew who Kiki was. She fluttered back and forth from sofa to chairs, plumping up pillows and poking a scatter of movie magazines into a tidy pile. She gestured toward the sofa, so Maggie and Kiki sat down.

"Billie!" Mrs. Martin called, "Billie, dear!" until finally a little knobby-kneed, string bean of a girl ran into the room. She stopped and stared at Maggie and Kiki as she pushed back a mass of tight blond curls from her eyes.

Mrs. Martin licked a finger and rubbed at a smudge on Billie's chin. "Stand up straight, dear," she murmured, and introduced her daughter.

As Kiki explained why they had come, Mrs. Martin's eyes grew wider and wider.

Finally she said, "You must be wrong, Mrs. Ledoux. Mr. Klinke emphasized over and over that experience was important, that it would help Billie to take nonpaying jobs just to get experience."

"They weren't nonpaying jobs," Kiki said. "Billie should have been paid, but Mr. Klinke kept the money."

"There must be an answer," Mrs. Martin said.

"There is. He was cheating you."

Mrs. Martin twisted her fingers together. "Oh, dear me, I find it so hard to believe." She leaned toward Kiki on the sofa. "Mr. Klinke has done so much for Billie."

For the first time Billie spoke. "He's going to make me famous."

"He's charging you for acting lessons, isn't he?" Maggie asked her.

"I need them. I don't know anything about acting," Billie said, "and I have to learn if I'm going to make lots of money and get famous."

"Now, now," her mother said as she reached over to pat Billie's knee, "you have a natural talent. Mr. Klinke said so."

Billie just shrugged. "I'd rather be a baseball player."

"Don't be ridiculous," her mother snapped. She leaned back and shook her head. "It's very hard to find an agent," she said to Kiki.

"A good, reputable agent, yes," Kiki answered. "But someone like Klinke won't help Billie." She eagerly leaned forward. "Mrs. Martin, if you and the Norrises and some of the other parents whom Klinke is cheating all get together, you could hire an attorney and—"

But Mrs. Martin gasped. "We couldn't do that!"

"Look—if it's a financial problem, a number of you could share the expense, and—"

"It's not that!" Mrs. Martin jumped to her feet and walked back and forth across the living room as though she were a windup doll making a path across the rug. "I suppose that finances would enter into it, but all that aside, the big problem is Billie's reputation!"

"I don't understand," Kiki said.

"Word gets around in Hollywood," Mrs. Martin explained. "If Billie were known to have brought suit against her agent, no one else would want to handle her."

"But Klinke's not a reputable agent."

"Billie's career means everything to her! We've given up so much and made so many sacrifices to provide her with the opportunity to—" Mrs. Martin interrupted herself as she stopped her pacing to face Kiki. She clasped her hands together under her chin and said, "Billie's every bit as talented as any other child in television or movies. And think how much money she could make. We could have a beautiful home, and lovely clothes, and a car that wouldn't be so old that it was always getting repaired, and—"

Mrs. Martin blinked rapidly, and Maggie knew she was going to interrupt herself and change subjects again. Maggie was right.

Mrs. Martin's voice dropped as though she were sharing secrets, and she said, "You know Timmy Blake, don't you?" Before Maggie or Kiki could answer, Mrs. Martin said, "Of course you do. Well, he got his start in Hollywood through Jerry Klinke."

"I don't think—" Maggie began, but Mrs. Martin continued.

"Oh yes, he did, but it just isn't well known. Mr. Klinke was Timmy Blake's agent for over a year and worked very hard to get him parts. Then, when Timmy Blake began to be known around Hollywood, without a word of gratitude he dumped Mr. Klinke and went with another agent. And that's the truth because Mr. Klinke told us so."

Maggie couldn't stand it another minute. "We know Timmy Blake," she said. "And Blake told us he'd never heard of Jerry Klinke."

"Ungrateful boy," Mrs. Martin said.

Maggie couldn't believe what she'd heard. "Blake was telling the truth. Mr. Klinke wasn't."

Mrs. Martin went back to squeezing her fingers together. Billie just slumped down on the sofa and looked bored.

"You'd be helping your own daughter as well as some of the other children who are signed up with Jerry Klinke," Kiki told Mrs. Martin.

But Mrs. Martin shook her head. "We can't," she said. "And you're going to get the same answer from other parents you talk to. Please understand. We can't do anything to hurt Billie's career as an actress."

"I could play baseball," Billie said.

Maggie and Kiki stood up at the same time and walked to the door.

"Thank you for your time," Kiki said.

"You do understand, don't you?" Mrs. Martin asked.

"I think so," Kiki said, and they left.

Maggie was glad that Kiki didn't want to talk much on the drive back to the Malibu Colony. Maggie had a lot to think about.

Her friend Truly was unhappy because she desperately wanted to be a successful actress. But Blake, who was already successful, didn't seem much happier. It was puzzling, and she planned to talk about it with Blake.

It was less than two minutes after Kiki had parked the car

and they had entered their home that the doorbell rang, and there was Blake. Maggie was still holding her package from Jax.

He leaned against the doorframe and beamed his gleaming Dick Dackery smile at Maggie. "Hi," he said. "Are you busy?"

"Save Dick Dackery for your fans," she teased. "I like Blake better."

He followed her into the living room saying, "Sometimes you confuse me. I don't understand it when you tell me that sometimes I'm Dick Dackery."

Roger and Kiki greeted Blake. "We were discussing going out to dinner," Roger said. "Apparently Kiki and Maggie were too busy today to get to the grocery store, so the alternative is someone else's cooking. Would you like to come with us, Blake?"

"Thanks," he said, "but I'll have to ask Mother, and of course it will depend on where you're planning to go."

"People mob him at Baskin-Robbins," Maggie explained.

"I had something else in mind besides Baskin-Robbins," her father said.

"Let me guess," Kiki said. "The Polo Lounge at the Beverly Hills Hotel again."

"No," Roger told her. "But I've made reservations there for Christmas dinner."

"I'll be there, too," Blake said. "Not in the Polo Lounge, but at a private party at the hotel. The producer of 'Dick and Doc Dackery' is entertaining a lot of people, and I have to show up in uniform and help entertain." He went on to talk about the people who'd be there, but Maggie tuned him out.

Like a quick snapshot, her mind was suddenly flooded with a bright picture of Grandma's kitchen, with her aunts and uncles and cousins crowding around the large table, which was laden with buttery rolls, shimmering cranberry sauce, huge heaps of mashed potatoes and candied yams, string beans and bowls of gravy, and on Grandma's special, gigantic platter a large, golden brown turkey. In her picture everyone was talking and laughing and filling their plates high.

But another snapshot followed: the elegant pink and green Polo Lounge as Maggie remembered it, with its attentive waiters and dignified diners. It was where film people went to be seen and where many business deals in the film industry were made. Maggie blinked back the quick tears that came to her eyes.

She didn't want to be here. She wished she were in Houston. Right now. Right this very minute. She was missing out on all the real Christmas fun because of her father. It was his fault!

"Margaret," she heard him say. "We don't know where your private thoughts are taking you, but you should have learned by now—when people are speaking to you, it's rude to daydream."

12

He went on without waiting for her to reply. "How about Trumps? Or Chasens? Or L'Escoffier? Do you have a choice?" he asked.

"Uh—no," Maggie mumbled. He wouldn't like to hear her real choice.

"Then how about L'Escoffier?" he said. "We haven't been there for a while, and it's quiet. Very nice."

"Yes, it is." Blake nodded. "I'll call Mother, if you don't mind."

He returned in a moment. "She told me to enjoy myself and remember to say thank you. She was really glad I'm going out because being on the set with me all day gave her a terrible headache." He strode toward the door. "I'll change as fast as I can and be right back."

As the door shut behind him, Maggie asked her father, "Do we have to dress up?"

Roger shrugged. "Of course we do." He paused as he looked at her carefully. "You did bring a few dressy dresses with you, didn't you?"

"Two," she said. "It's okay. I won't disgrace you."

"That's not what I meant," he said. "Do you need more clothes? I'm sure that Kiki will be glad to take you shopping."

"No. In Houston I hardly ever dress up much. None of the kids do. Besides, Kiki and I already went shopping."

Roger looked pleased and glanced at the bag she was still holding. "So I see. What did you get?"

Maggie fished into the bag and pulled out one of the T-shirts—the green one.

He looked a little startled, then said, "Oh. That's what you young people like to wear?"

"Oh, it's not for me," Maggie said. "It's for Grandma."

"Your grandmother? Surely you could find something more appropriate for a grandmother."

Maggie was irritated. "She's not *a* grandmother. She's *Grandma*," she began, but Kiki made shooing motions at her.

"Hurry and get dressed," Kiki said. "I'm getting terribly hungry!"

Maggie ran into her bedroom and pulled out the blue dress she had brought to Houston with her at the beginning of last summer and hadn't worn since. She washed her face and brushed her hair and slipped the dress over her head.

She looked at herself in the mirror and laughed. The dress, which was once snug around the waist, hung loose. That part was wonderful. The bad part, one that wouldn't make her father too happy, was that the dress was now decidedly too short. "I've been growing!" Maggie said.

She opened her door and poked her head out. Kiki was just coming down the hallway, the skirt of her lavender silk dress billowing out behind her. "Kiki!" Maggie whispered. "Can you come in here? I've got a problem."

Kiki hurried into Maggie's room.

Maggie stood stiffly, hands held out. "Look. My dress is too short."

"How about the other one?" Kiki asked. She pulled it from

the closet and held it up to Maggie. It wasn't any longer than the one she had on.

"Obviously you need a new dress right this minute," Kiki said, "and since shopping that quickly would be impossible, let me see what I can find in my closet. Take that one off. I'll be right back."

By the time Maggie had pulled off the dress and hung it up, Kiki had returned. She held up a simply designed, white wool dress with an open collar and large patch pockets on the full skirt. "The cleaners shrank this," she said. "I was going to take it back and complain, but I was busy and forgot to. Now I'm glad that I did because I think it will fit you."

"It's beautiful," Maggie said, "but I'm sure it will be too small for me."

"Try it," Kiki said, as she helped Maggie pull it over her head. She straightened the shoulders and pulled up the long back zipper. "It fits perfectly! Oh, Maggie, wait till you see yourself in the mirror!"

Maggie took a step toward the mirror, but Kiki whirled her around. "Wait a minute. I'm not through." She picked up a pink-flowered scarf, which she had thrown onto the bed, and tied it around Maggie's waist. Then she looped a long strand of tiny pink and gold beads around Maggie's neck. "Now you can look! You're gorgeous!"

Maggie was surprised by the girl who looked back at her in the mirror. "I look older," she said. "It must be the dress."

Kiki put her hands on Maggie's shoulders. "Granted, the dress makes you look older than the shirts and shorts and jeans you usually wear, but much of that older look comes from the fact that you're growing up."

Maggie leaned to peer more closely into the mirror. "I've got cheekbones! I used to have just a plain old round face, but look, Kiki! There are shadows under my cheekbones!"

Feeling strange and shivery, Maggie stepped back from the mirror and hugged her elbows tightly. "I'd like to go back to Grandma's and be just the way I was," she whispered.

"Don't be afraid of growing up," Kiki said. "You're going to do it beautifully."

"It has to be the dress," Maggie blurted out. "It's not my kind of dress, and I don't feel like myself. It's as though I'm trying to be you." Suddenly embarrassed, Maggie quickly added, "I didn't mean to be rude. You're very kind to lend me your dress. I like it. Really! I should have thanked you. I—"

Kiki laughed. "Hold it, Maggie. I understand. Wear the dress tonight. Tomorrow morning we'll go shopping for one you'll feel comfortable in. You can wear the new dress on Christmas."

"The day after tomorrow," Maggie said.

The telephone rang, and Roger called, "Kiki? It's for you. A Detective Bill Hartley. Is there some reason a detective is calling you?"

"There's no problem," Kiki called. "I'll tell you all about it later." She said to Maggie, "I wonder why Bill is calling." She picked up the phone on the table by Maggie's bed.

The conversation didn't take long. Kiki kept saying, "Uh-huh," and nodding, until finally she said, "Thanks, Bill. That information should help. I'll let you know how it all comes out."

She put down the receiver and said, "Bill got the results of the computer check on Jerry Klinke. He's been arrested twice for tricking and cheating people."

"As an agent?"

"No. He was involved in selling real estate in Colorado that wasn't what and where it was supposed to be."

"How is that information going to help Truly and her father?"

"I'm not sure," Kiki said. "Bill suggested again that they'd need a lawyer."

"Kiki? Margaret?" Roger called. "Are you ready?"

"Coming," Kiki said and hurried from the bedroom. Maggie took another quick look in the mirror as she followed Kiki.

"Lovely," Roger said with enthusiasm, but Maggie saw that he was smiling at Kiki and not at her.

However, Blake perked up when he saw Maggie. She took it as a compliment until he mumbled in her ear as they walked to the garage, "Now who's trying to be somebody else?"

"I am not!" Maggie snapped. It wasn't fair! Why should Blake assume she was pretending?

Maggie sat near the car door and deliberately stared out the window as they drove from the Malibu Colony and entered the traffic on the Pacific Coast Highway. Blake didn't know how wrong he was. How could she try to be someone else when she didn't know who she was in the first place? She hardly remembered the girl she was a year ago—the pudgy, unhappy Margaret Ledoux who hated boarding school and couldn't get along with her father. She had found a grandmother to love and friends to have fun with and had turned into Maggie Ledoux. Now here she was, wearing someone else's dress, suddenly taller and slimmer and unable to get her mind off the girl she had glimpsed in the mirror. Only one thing hadn't changed. She still couldn't get along with her father.

Blake slid over on the car seat until he was next to her and took her hand. "Don't be mad," he said. "I was just kidding. You look so—different. A lot older. You know, you're very pretty."

Maggie tried to keep from blushing, but she couldn't. So she tried to cover up by shrugging as though she didn't believe Blake for a minute. "People don't call me pretty," she mumbled.

"I do."

She looked at him carefully. Dick Dackery was nowhere in sight. Blake was the one who had said it. "Thanks," she answered, and grinned at him, suddenly aware that the evening air was warmer, the water gleamed more brightly, and the sky, shot with sunset streaks of orange and gold, was truly spectacular.

Finally Roger asked, "Okay, what's the story about the phone call from the detective? Traffic ticket?"

"Traffic ticket!" Kiki laughed. "Maggie, let's tell them what we found out today," she said, and began reciting the details without pausing for breath.

She still hadn't finished when Roger pulled up in front of the Beverly Hills Hilton. "To be continued in the restaurant," Roger said.

The car was whisked away by a uniformed attendant, and the four of them walked into the lobby of the hotel and to the elevators. Maggie was conscious of a couple of people staring at Blake. Two teenaged girls even turned around to gawk.

"Is it always like this?" she whispered to Blake as the elevator doors closed.

"This isn't bad," he said.

"Doesn't it bother you? When people are staring, don't you wonder if maybe you've got mustard on your chin, or a spot on your shirt, or a hole in your pants?"

His eyebrows dipped into a frown for an instant as he apparently thought about her question. Then he shrugged and said, "I don't know what it would be like any other way."

Evergreen garlands, decorated with gold and white bows, were twined through the ornate wrought-iron doors of the restaurant, and large rose and pink bouquets in tall silver compotes centered each table.

They were seated at a table near the wide windows. It was dark enough now to see the lights of the city twinkling and winking like the lights on Grandma's Christmas tree. Maggie took a deep breath and shook her head. No! She wouldn't think about Grandma now. It hurt too much.

She hid behind the menu the waiter had handed her and concentrated on what she wanted to eat. She wished that the restaurant served hamburgers and french fries, but of course it didn't. She ordered a veal dish with artichoke hearts, handed back her menu, and prepared to listen as Kiki finished the story.

After Kiki had told them what Mrs. Martin said, Blake scowled. "That's not true! I've never even met this Jerry Klinke. I wonder how many people he's told that lie to!"

"I'm surprised that Mrs. Martin would believe it," Kiki said.

"I'm not," Roger said. "Some people believe anything that's convenient to believe. They're greedy for money and fame and blind to everything else. Mrs. Martin's a good example of the kind of people who fall right into the hands of con artists like Klinke. Mr. Norris is another one."

The waiter appeared with salads, and no one spoke until after he had left. Then Maggie said, "Don't say that about Mr. Norris, Daddy! He isn't greedy. He was trying to help Truly."

Roger buttered a roll and took a bite, chewing it carefully before he answered. "There's an old expression, Margaret. 'Let the sucker beware.'"

"That's an awful thing to say! Mr. Norris believes in Truly. She wants to be an actress, and he's helping her."

"Then he should talk her into going to school and preparing for college and a job she can handle. I'd be willing to bet that she doesn't have the special talent an acting career would take. Hollywood is full of kids who'll never make it."

Maggie was furious. She dropped her fork and gripped the

edge of the table. Blake took her other hand and held it tightly, but she resisted the pressure of his fingers. She knew her voice was rising, but she couldn't stop. "Daddy!" Maggie exclaimed. "You could help Truly! But you won't! Because you don't care enough to help!"

13

Roger's voice was cold. "Margaret, behave yourself. Please remember that you are in public."

Maggie slumped against the back of her chair. Of course she should have remembered. The girl she saw this evening in the mirror would have. She took a long breath and willed herself to calm down. Then she raised her head and looked at her father.

"I'm sorry," she said. "You're right. I was acting like a child."

Roger's eyes widened. Before he could say anything, Maggie continued. "You and I are two separate people, with two ways of looking at things. Just because something is important to me, I have no right to expect that it would be important to you. I shouldn't have lost my temper."

Blake squeezed her fingers, and she was surprised to discover that he was still holding her hand. Kiki smiled at her, and it was like Grandma's smile when she was especially proud of Maggie.

"Well, Margaret," Roger said. He cleared his throat and began again. "I can understand how you feel about your friend.

It's just that I see so many, many people desperately wanting acting careers and so many who are taken in by crooks, and—" He shrugged. "I'll give it some thought. Perhaps there might be something I can do."

"Thank you, Daddy!"

"I told you what Detective Hartley told us." Kiki sighed. "I wish there were just some way that we could talk a few of Klinke's clients into hiring an attorney."

"But they don't have enough money," Maggie said. "Or, like Mrs. Martin, they're afraid to."

Blake spoke up. "Maybe I could talk to Mrs. Martin. Maybe she'd realize that Klinke had lied to her about me if I told her so."

Roger shook his head. "She might and she might not. Probably not. What you really want," he began, looking at Kiki. Then he suddenly stopped and turned to Maggie. "What you want is legal action against Jerry Klinke. Is that right?"

"Yes," Maggie said.

"I know a very good young attorney," Roger said. "I'll give you his name. And tell him that I'll pick up the bills for whatever work he has to do."

Kiki kissed Roger's cheek, and Maggie grinned at him. "Thank you, Daddy! We'll call him right now!"

"No! Not right now!" Roger tried to look stern, but a smile tilted one corner of his mouth. "In the first place, his office would be closed at this hour. And in the second place, we are going to have a relaxed, enjoyable dinner."

"I'll certainly agree to that," Kiki said. "I'll call him tomorrow morning."

Maggie nodded in agreement. She did enjoy the dinner, and it was fun to hear Blake tell about some of the funny things that happened on the "Dick and Doc Dackery" set. But she was so excited and so impatient to hear what the attorney would tell them that it was terribly hard to wait until the next morning.

Maggie woke up so early that the sky was still gray and the ocean a dull mirror. She made herself some buttered toast, poured a glass of orange juice, tugged on a sweater, and sat out on the deck, letting the breeze shiver through her hair.

When a voice spoke below her, she jumped, nearly spilling the juice.

"Have you got enough breakfast for two?"

"Blake! I didn't see you. Come on up."

Blake took the stairs two at a time, following her into the kitchen. He helped carry his juice and another plate of toast out to the deck and pulled up a chair next to Maggie.

"I thought I was the only one in the city up this early," Maggie said.

"I'm used to getting up early," Blake told her. He took a large bite of toast and mumbled, "When we're filming, I have to be on the set by six."

"That's awfully early to start work," Maggie said. "Does that mean that you get through early, too?"

"We work a twelve- to sixteen-hour day—counting the time I spend with my teacher."

"Are you the only one in the class?"

"Usually, unless there are other kids in one of the scripts."

"Don't you get lonely? Don't you ever wish you were back in a regular school?"

Blake took a long drink of orange juice before he put down the glass and looked at her. "I've never been in a regular school. I don't really want to be. I don't think I'd like it. I wouldn't know what to do or say with the other kids in my class."

"You know what to say to me."

"That's different. I know you. We're friends."

Maggie smiled at the word. She liked the sound of it. She liked being Blake's friend.

The glass door slid open, and Kiki stepped through. "You got a head start," she said. "Out watching the sun rise?"

Maggie looked up to see that the sky was now flooded with color. She jumped up. "Can we call the attorney now?"

"Give him a chance to get to his office," Kiki said.

"Whatever you're going to do, I'd like to help," Blake told them.

"Thanks," Maggie said.

He looked down at the deck as he continued, "I—I asked Mom if I could do something for Truly, like try to get her a part or help her find a real agent. But she said that she didn't want me to get involved, that there were too many people like Truly in Hollywood and too many like Jerry Klinke." Blake raised his head and looked into Maggie's eyes. "No matter what Mom thinks, I'm going to help Truly if I can. Just let me know what I can do."

Maggie knew that her smile was enough answer for Blake, but Kiki said, "Good for you, Blake. Right now we don't know what we'll be doing, but if we need you, we'll certainly call 'help.' "

It occurred to Maggie later that there were many times during the day that she would have liked to have called "help!"

The morning was filled with legal matters that seemed to take much too long. Kiki and Maggie met with Jonathan Browne, the attorney; came back with Mr. Norris and Truly for another talk; and listened to Mr. Browne's explanation of how things would be accomplished. He would prepare and file a complaint in court on behalf of Mr. Norris, as guardian for Truly, against Jerry Klinke.

He would also request the court clerk to issue a summons to Mr. Klinke.

"What does that mean?" Maggie asked. "Will Mr. Klinke be arrested?"

Mr. Browne shook his head. "No. It just means that he is informed that court action will be taken against him, that he'll be the defendant in the case when it comes to trial." As though he anticipated Maggie's next question, he quickly added, "The summons can be delivered even before the complaint is filed. Even though the sheriff's office usually delivers summons, anyone over the age of twenty-one, who is not a party to the action, can deliver it."

Kiki sat up straight. "I'm twenty-one. Let me deliver it."

"You don't have to," Mr. Browne told her.

"But I want to," Kiki said. "Maggie and I paid Klinke one visit in disguise. Now he'll have a chance to meet the real Ledouxs!"

It took a while to obtain the summons and go through all the legal red tape, but finally Kiki tucked the envelope into her handbag and smiled at Maggie. "Next stop—Jerry Klinke's office!" she said.

"He'll be surprised!" It was hard for Maggie to wait. Traffic was heavy and slow, and it seemed to take hours until Kiki drove into the small parking lot behind the old stucco building where Jerry Klinke had his office.

Maggie and Kiki raced up the stairs, threw open the door with Klinke's name on it in gold, and burst into his office.

Lois's surprised stare soon changed to a scowl. "Mr. Klinke isn't in," she snapped at them.

"When will he be back?" Kiki asked.

"He's on a long holiday," Lois said. She picked up a magazine and pretended to be reading it.

"But he can't be!" Maggie said. She took a couple of steps

toward the door to Klinke's office, opened it, and peered inside.

Lois slapped the magazine down on the desk and said, "He's not in there. You won't find him. And whatever you have in mind won't work!"

Kiki leaned on the desk, her face close to Lois's face. "What are you talking about?" she asked in such a chilling voice that even Maggie was startled.

Lois cringed. "Mrs. Martin called us," she said, her voice tight and scratchy. "She told us who you are and how you were trying to stir up trouble."

Kiki stood up straight and smoothed down her skirt. "Then there's no point in our being here, Maggie," she said.

Maggie stepped back so suddenly that she lost her balance and plopped into a chair. "But, Kiki, we can't give up!" she cried. "What are we going to do?"

14

Kiki didn't speak until they were out of the building, and then she surprised Maggie by saying, "We're going to buy you a dress to wear tomorrow when we go out for Christmas dinner."

Maggie stopped on the sidewalk in the shade of one of the metal Christmas trees that were attached to the lampposts. She stared at Kiki. "But what should we do about Mr. Klinke?"

"It's a sure thing that we aren't going to find him at his office," Kiki said.

"I know. Lois said he was out of town."

"I hardly believe that. When we had our appointment with Klinke, he mentioned that he was working on so many deals that he was distracted. He wouldn't run out on anything that might make some money for him."

"Then where is he?"

"Obviously, he's hiding from us," Kiki said. "Come on, Maggie. Let's go to the car. We can't just stand here in the middle of the sidewalk."

They were in the car, and Kiki had driven out to the boulevard before she continued. "We may not find Klinke for days.

He's going to try to avoid us. But I'll keep the summons in my handbag, and sooner or later we'll meet up with him."

"Just accidentally?" Maggie looked out at the tourists who were clustered in large groups in front of Mann's Chinese Theater, staring at the many movie stars' footprints and hand-prints, which were imbedded in the cement.

"No. We'll try to figure out where he might be and hunt for him." Kiki edged around a tour bus that was temporarily double-parked and turned down La Brea Boulevard. "But for now," Kiki added, "we're going to buy you a Christmas dress."

Maggie slumped back against the seat. She didn't want to buy a dress. She didn't want to have a formal Christmas dinner at the Polo Lounge. Tomorrow was Christmas, and she wished she could be spending it with Grandma. She felt like pouting and fussing and making everyone around her as unhappy as she was.

A few months ago she would have done it, Maggie knew. But things had changed. Or was she the one who had changed? From the corners of her eyes she glanced at Kiki, whose tan profile was serene and beautiful. She could understand why her father had fallen in love with Kiki. Maggie liked to be with Kiki, too.

"I don't wear dresses very often," Maggie said.

"But tomorrow," Kiki answered, "it will please your father very much if you do wear a lovely dress."

"Oh, I didn't mean that I don't want to," Maggie said quickly. As Kiki turned to glance at her, Maggie shyly added, "I meant that I haven't thought much about dresses, so I hoped that you'd help me pick one out. I guess I need your advice."

Kiki smiled with pleasure. "I'd love to give it. We'll find you something gorgeous, maybe in red. Red would be perfect with your coloring. You'll be beautiful in red."

And red it was. As Maggie looked into the dressing room

mirror at the girl wearing the red velvet dress with the wide lace collar, again she seemed to see a different person.

Maybe she was a different person.

"Kiki," she asked, "do we have time for more shopping? I'd like to get something for Truly and for Blake."

"Have anything in mind?" Kiki asked.

"Yes," Maggie said. "I'm going to get them stationery."

"That's a good type of gift," Kiki said, and after Maggie had changed into her shirt and jeans and the dress was paid for and boxed, she led Maggie to the store's stationery department.

Maggie chose a box of pale blue for Truly and a heavy cream kind for Blake. Then, as Kiki strolled to the end of the counter to look at the display, Maggie quickly thrust a box of delicate pink stationery and a box of beige into the saleswoman's hands. "Could you gift-wrap them, please?" Maggie asked. She emptied the contents of her wallet and was relieved to find that she had enough to pay for her purchases.

In a few moments Maggie accepted the bag and twenty cents change and joined Kiki. "All taken care of," she said, delighted with her sudden inspiration.

They made their way through the heavy crowd of last-minute Christmas Eve shoppers and began to drive home.

Maggie was surprised to find Blake there, waiting for her.

"Merry Christmas," he said.

"It's not Christmas until tomorrow."

"I know, but tomorrow I'll be working most of the day, so I wanted to give you your Christmas present early." He held out a flat box that was wrapped in gold paper.

Maggie grinned with delight. She fished into the bag she was carrying and pulled out a box wrapped with red-and-green metallic stripes. "And I've got one for you!"

"Open yours now."

"But it's not Christmas."

"I've got a good idea," Kiki said. "I can't wait another minute to open presents. Why don't I make some omelets for dinner, and we'll all sit around the tree afterward and open our presents then? I hope you'll be able to stay, Blake."

"I'll check with Mom," Blake said, "but I'm sure I can. She's got friends coming over for cocktails. She won't miss me."

While he was on the telephone, Maggie pulled the other packages from her bag and put them under the tree. They were wrapped alike, but luckily the person who had wrapped them had stuck notes on the bottom describing the contents.

The evening was fun, especially when Blake and Maggie found they had given each other the very same stationery. Roger had given Maggie a gold bracelet, and Kiki's gift—which made Maggie squeal with delight—was a new stereo and a big gift certificate with a national chain of music stores. The cookies that Maggie had made and that had been wrapped tightly in foil by Grandma were highly praised and quickly eaten.

Grandma. Another picture flashed into Maggie's mind: All of them around Grandma's tree. Debbie and Jason would be hopping up and down, wanting to tear open their packages, and— She forced the picture from her mind. She was here. This was now. And she was going to enjoy Christmas Eve with her father and Kiki and Blake.

The warm glow lasted, even through her Christmas morning telephone conversation with Grandma and the others. Debbie screamed a long list of presents everyone had received while the others used the extension to shout happy Christmas wishes and tell her they missed her. Finally the others got off the line, and she was able to talk to Grandma.

"How is your friend, Truly?" Grandma asked, so Maggie told her what had happened.

"Well then," Grandma said, "you'll need to find Mr. Klinke."

"We don't know where to look," Maggie said.

"Hmmm." Grandma thought a moment. Then she said, "In the mystery novels I read, sometimes the detective manages to get a note to a criminal asking him to meet him. Maybe, if Mr. Klinke thought you and Kiki would just talk to him, he'd—"

But a wonderful idea popped into Maggie's mind. "Thanks, Grandma!" she said. "I think I know what to do!"

"Maggie, be sure to talk to Kiki about it before—"

"It's okay, Grandma. I won't do anything foolish."

"It would be better if you'd—"

"I promise I'll tell Dad about it. I love you, Grandma!" Maggie said.

"I love you, too," Grandma said.

Before Grandma could say another word, Maggie shouted, "Merry Christmas! I'll see you in a week!" and hung up the receiver.

She could hardly wait until her father woke up. In about an hour he padded into the kitchen in his bare feet, rubbing his eyes.

"I've made your coffee already," Maggie announced. "And I'll scramble some eggs for you and make you toast—anything you want. And while you eat, I'll tell you how we can find Jerry Klinke."

Roger poured a cup of coffee and sat across the table from Maggie. "The coffee will be enough, Margaret. Tell me what you have in mind."

"Send him a message through his answering service," Maggie said. "Tell him to meet you this afternoon in the Polo Lounge. Then, when he shows up, Kiki can serve him with the summons."

"He won't come. Remember, he knows your names are Ledoux."

"Oh." Maggie slumped in her chair. "It seemed like such a good idea."

"Maybe it is," Roger said. "After all, it involves a simple serving of a summons—nothing that could disrupt a quiet, pleasant dinner." He looked at his watch and pushed back his chair. "I can get my assistant to call and use his name. Whether it works or not, we'll give your idea a try."

Maggie jumped up and hugged her father. "Thank you!" As he hugged her back, she said, "It's strange, Dad, but I feel as though I'm just beginning to know you."

"I feel the same way about you," he said.

"Kiki said that we're very much alike."

For an instant he looked surprised. Then he said, "Maybe she's right. Maybe that's been our problem."

"It doesn't have to be," Maggie said.

Roger opened his mouth, then closed it, as though he didn't know what to say next. Quickly he straightened and walked to the phone. "I'll call Art now. We'll see what happens."

"It's going to be hard to wait."

Roger chuckled. "Poor little Margaret. You seem to have inherited my impatience, too."

The rose carpet that lined the outdoor entrance to the Beverly Hills Hotel was flanked by huge clay pots of red poinsettias, and the posts that held the green-and-white striped canopy were decorated with lighted wreaths. The Polo Lounge was banked with white poinsettias, and in the middle of each pink tablecloth was a vase with fresh pink rosebuds.

At Roger's request a circular booth near the front door of the restaurant had been reserved for them. Maggie positioned herself so that she could get a clear view of the doorway without being spotted by anyone who arrived at the door.

A waitress brought them menus. "I'm glad you chose the Lounge, Mr. Ledoux," she said. "It's nearly filled, but not as crowded as the ballroom. I don't know how many hundreds of people will be served dinner in there today."

They ordered and were soon served, but Jerry Klinke didn't show up.

The waitress took away their plates and brought snowballs with fudge sauce, while Maggie fidgeted. Roger looked at his watch and said, "Sorry, Margaret. Either Klinke didn't get the message or he didn't choose to come."

"I wish he had come," Kiki said. "I've got that summons right here in my handbag."

Maggie noticed a few heads turning toward the doorway. Dick Dackery, complete with blue uniform and helmet, walked into the Polo Lounge, followed by Santa Claus. Santa stopped to chat at a few tables, but Blake came directly to the Ledoux table.

Before he could even say "hello," two giggly children rushed over to him. "Hi, Dick," one of them said, while the other ducked her head shyly.

"It's him!" Kiki gasped.

"We know it's him," one of the little girls said.

"Klinke! He's standing in the doorway, looking around the room!"

Maggie leaned so far around Blake to get a look at the doorway that she lost her balance and fell out of the booth. Just then Klinke glanced in her direction. His eyes widened, his mouth made a surprised "O," and he quickly turned from the doorway.

Maggie scrambled to her feet. "That's Klinke!" she shouted to Blake. "Catch him!"

Klinke made a quick left and ran through the door to the gardens of the hotel. Blake, Maggie, and Kiki dashed after him. Santa and the two little girls ran with them, and Maggie could hear her father in the rear as he shouted to Klinke to stop.

They dashed past the courtyard and were on the paths to the cottages by the time Blake caught up with Klinke. He grabbed one of Klinke's arms, and as Klinke struggled to get away, Maggie grabbed the other. Kiki dashed up, waved the summons in his face, and stuffed it into his shirt pocket.

Klinke began to struggle harder, but Santa Claus ran toward them so fast that it was hard for him to stop. Santa tripped over the two little girls and plowed into Klinke, knocking all of them off their feet.

Maggie, who landed in a flower bed, looked up to see a crowd of wide-eyed faces staring at her. Apparently a number of people had joined the run, thinking it was some kind of Christmas entertainment.

The hotel's security chief stepped up and, after Roger explained the situation, took Jerry Klinke by the arm.

"Look," Klinke hissed at Roger. "We can work something out, can't we? You want the Norrises to get their money back. Okay. And I'll drop the charges against Norris."

"There are others involved besides the Norris family," Roger said firmly.

"I said we'll work things out. I don't want any trouble. I'll cooperate."

"Our attorney's card is stapled to the envelope with the summons in it," Kiki told him. "Make an appointment with him, and we'll see if you mean what you're saying."

"I will. I do." Klinke brushed himself off and hurried away, shooting quick glances over his shoulder as though he were going to be chased again at any moment. The crowd, deciding the entertainment was over, wandered off.

But Maggie was so excited that she bounced up and down. "We did it!" she cried. "Blake, you were wonderful!"

"I wanted to help, and I did!" Blake took off his helmet, and Maggie could see his eyes shining. "This is the first time I've ever done something all on my own! And I caught him! I did it myself!" Suddenly Blake leaned over and kissed Maggie.

Maggie smiled at him. It was Blake who kissed her and not Dick Dackery. She liked his kiss. She liked Blake *very* much. She hoped that sometime in the future he'd kiss her again!

Roger smiled. "It looks as though this life is almost as exciting for you as your other one has been, Margaret."

Maggie put an arm around his waist. "I don't have two lives, Dad. I have one, and both parts of it are wonderful. I love living with Grandma, but I also love you and Kiki. And I have friends to love in both places. That's why I gave all of you stationery for Christmas. I want you to write to me often until I come back for another visit. Because I want very much to come."

"I'm proud of you, Margaret," her father said.

Maggie shook her head. "I have one life, Dad. Remember? And that means I have one name. Please, from now on call me Maggie. The name Margaret belonged to another girl, a not very happy girl." She hugged Roger tightly and said, "I *am* happy as Maggie, so for the rest of my life I want to be called Maggie. I'm going to be Maggie forevermore."

11113

F
NIX

Nixon, Joan Lowery.

Maggie forevermore.